Venom Wars of the Desert Realm

Venom Wars of the Desert Realm

ELIAS,

FOLLOW THE LIGHT!

Michael C. Baumann

ISBN: 1546835954
ISBN-13: 9781546835950
Library of Congress Control Number: 2017908490
CreateSpace Independent Publishing Platform
North Charleston, South Carolina

To my children: you are my heroes.

One

A column of frogs silently scaled the vertical walls of a giant mesa that towered out of the rolling hills of the Red Desert. The moon was almost full, and the sky was alive with stars. Although the sun had been hidden for hours, the earth still held its heat deep into this night. Frogs liked heat, especially these. The twisting line hopped upward in unison as it made its way toward a flickering light near the very top of the formation. The frogs were careful to avoid the lonely ironwoods and cacti that somehow grew from tiny cracks in the steep walls. Eons of wind and weather had worn the red rock smooth, exposing the layers of time that had been stacked upon one another.

Two torches hung near the opening, casting dancing shadows around the hollow. Inside the cavern, Aridin nervously paced in slow circles, his talons clicking on the floor. He was grand, the largest of all the eagles that flew in the desert and quite possibly anywhere else on earth. Deep-golden-brown plumage covered him completely, except for speckled tan feathers that ran down the underlining of his broad wings. Sparra's eyes smiled as she looked at her husband. Both were excited and a bit nervous as they waited for the arrival of their firstborn, now most likely just days away. These were not just any raptors tucked away in a lofty home; they were the royal family of the Desert Realm. Aridin, the eagle king, was beloved by those he watched over. He was powerful, always fair, and above all, fearless. He had done much in the fight for peace. Sparra was brave like her husband and was known everywhere for her compassion and care for those in need.

Aridin's heart warmed as he looked at the egg that lay in the sturdy nest resting at the back of their royal lair. The egg was their son, the unborn prince, the Oonakestree. Aridin felt the goodness that grew inside the spotted shell; it was the same goodness he felt when he looked at his wife.

Sparra was beautiful. Her feathers were much lighter than Aridin's. She was also much smaller than he was—barely half his size. She continued to tidy up their home, scattering dust and small pebbles with quick flits of her wings. She suddenly stopped her cleaning when she saw something move near the entrance of their home. A single frog had hopped inside. It had dead gray skin, with two bright-yellow lines that criss-crossed on its back, forming a bumpy, asymmetrical X. She froze with fear, and her eyes widened. Before she could speak, dozens more frogs had joined the first. They continued their way in and lined up in uneven rows. Curved and jagged fangs jutted from the frogs' mouths in all directions.

She felt light headed and started to sway; the movement of the yellow *X*s had a dizzying effect on her. "Aridin?" Sparra whispered to her husband, but her eyes were still locked on the lines of now-spinning yellow *X*s.

He turned and saw the small army of frogs. "Sparra!"

His words snapped her out of the trance, and she turned toward him. "Aridin?"

"Come to me." He stepped to her as he spoke.

"What do they want?" she whispered as she backed into his protective wings.

A hollow, wispy voice rose from behind the line of frogs. "They want nothing. These stupid creatures only do as I command them."

Sparra and Aridin knew that voice. It was Eelion, the great snake; he was one of the most powerful and dangerous of the Venomous Ones. Brown and red symmetrical scales formed diamond patterns that layered across his ecru back. His head was large and triangular; his long, forked black tongue darted in and out. His tail ended with a dozen or so white-and-black bony rattles that were stacked on one another; it swayed behind him but did not make a sound.

Many years ago, when Eelion had chosen to accept the way of the Venom, it had not only made him deadly but had also made him grow far bigger than any snake the desert had ever seen. His power and size gave him the ability to scale the steep face of the king's rocky castle, just as his stupid frogs had.

He hissed, "However, if you want to know what *I* want, it's right behind you!" Eelion turned his evil eyes toward the nest that held the Oonakestree. "I want your boy, dear King."

Shtk, shtk, shtk, shtk, shtk, shtk, shtk, shtk. His rattle came alive. The frogs parted, and Eelion slithered his way deeper into their home.

Aridin leaped out in front of Sparra, his long, curved talons chipped into the rock floor. He extended his wings and let out a long shrill screech, causing the X-marked frogs to all take jumps and stumble back. The last row fell out over the edge to the ground below.

Eelion quickly coiled up, and his rattle popped again. *Shtk, shtk, shtk, shtk, shtk.*

Four frogs stepped out from the lines, balancing something across their backs; it was a long, jagged tool made of bone.

Aridin looked down at the device. "This is a violation of the truce. Attacking us will bring an end to peace."

Eelion smiled at the king. He was not here for peace. "So naïve for such a great leader."

His rattle stopped, and his fanged frogs sprang toward them and began to violently snap at any piece of the birds they could.

Aridin and Sparra killed many of Eelion's attacking henchmen with slashes from their sharp talons. They flapped their wings, sending frogs flying in all directions around the cave. Some smashed horribly against the stone walls, whereas others were tossed out of the hollow.

Sparra stumbled toward her king and, with a gasp, pled, "Aridin—"

A single frog hung from her neck; its jagged teeth had made their way through the layer of feathers. She fell to the ground, and her breathing became short and quick.

"No!" Aridin exclaimed. Just as he turned his attention to Sparra, one of the last remaining frogs leaped at him and clamped down on his neck, injecting him with a paralyzing poison. He staggered in a half circle, trying to fight the effects, before he finally dropped to the ground next to Sparra. The king and queen now lay helplessly on the ground, facing each other as dread came over them like an icy wave. They both knew what Eelion was after.

"Well done, you stupid little creatures."

He slithered toward the paralyzed birds. His rattle popped, and the frogs carried the bone tool over to him. Eelion lowered his fanged face directly in front of Aridin's, his darting tongue almost touching the king's beak.

"The Oonakestree belongs to the Venom!" he hissed. "Your *son* now belongs to the Venom. The desert belongs to the Venom!"

He snapped his head back toward the nest. The thin slits of his pupils widened as he shifted his focus to the Oonakestree. Aridin was thankful Sparra's back was to the nest so she would not have to see what was going to happen to their son. Eelion unhinged his jaw and swallowed the speckled egg whole. The egg moved downward through his body as he slithered across the floor back toward the opening of the lair.

With prideful glee and an evil grin, he hissed, "Make sure he does *not* fly again! The feathered ones will give up once they know their king has been defeated and will no longer fly."

Sparra would not be saved from seeing this horror. Tears filled her eyes as the four frogs, two at each end, brought the barbaric device toward Aridin's head.

"Do not be afraid, my love," Aridin said as he fought to keep his eyes open.

The frogs positioned their cutting device to the right side of the king's neck, where his wing met his body. Two frogs sat balanced atop each end of the bone saw. Their weight pushed down on the tool, and it began to slice into his feathers.

With a single pop of Eelion's rattle, one of the frogs leaped straight up off the end of the tool. It landed, pushing it downward, cutting even further into the thick layer of Aridin's golden feathers. The frog's force also launched the two others off the opposite end of the tool. They landed, and the blade continued to work. The frogs hopped and flipped in an acrobatic motion that continued to drive the blade downward, until it finally cut clean through Aridin's shoulder. His wing slid down his back and fell softly onto the floor. Sparra lost consciousness when she saw the small white bone jutting out of her husband's side. The frogs croaked in unison as they completed their job and brought the bloodied bone tool away. Eelion smiled, and his tail came alive again, as if applauding his frogs. Only thirteen frogs had survived the melee. They fell into a semicircle around their leader.

Eelion turned away from the fallen royal family and looked down upon his remaining soldiers. "Well done, little vermin."

He then pushed his way toward the exit, sliding through the piles of dead frogs that littered the floor. He stopped before his careful descent, looking back at the two motionless birds.

"Farewell, Aridin. Your reign as king is over." Eelion sneered at him and then turned back to his amphibious gang. "Take his wing. That is *my* trophy."

Two

With sure, steady paces, Honu made his way up the final steep incline of a narrow path that twisted up to a bluff overlooking the beach of an enormous lake. It was known as the Great Lake of the Desert Realm. It was several miles wide in every direction, and most believed it was equally deep. The Roos River was wide and slow moving and fed freshwater into the Great Lake from the east while two smaller rivers, the Nell and the Briz, flowed out of its western banks through two narrow and rocky canyons.

Honu was large but remarkably agile for a tortoise that was almost eight hundred years old. His legs were sturdy, rugged, and covered with tight patterns of thick oval and oblong scales. His claws were long and curved and provided sure footing up the winding trail. His enormous shell looked as if it were made of stone.

All eyes of those gathered on the sandy cove of the Great Lake were fixed on him as he made his way to the top of the rocky bluff.

"Brothers and sisters of the Desert Realm, my heart is lifted by seeing you all here. I only wish it were under brighter circumstances. Hillmaken has found and unearthed the Venom Stone and has again been using it to build an army. And now he has attacked our king and queen."

He paused for a moment and took in a deep, slow breath. His voice remained strong and calm as he prepared to deliver more bad news. "The Venomous Ones have taken the Oonakestree. They will attempt to fulfill their dark prophecies and convert all who dwell in the desert. They mean to bring war to us."

A murmur of worry quickly spread through the gathering of animals. There was concern, because Honu, who had not been seen for over seventy years, now stood before them and delivered dark and dangerous news. He was one of the oldest and wisest of the Elders of the Desert Realm; many had only heard stories of him but had never seen him with their own eyes.

A soft voice rose from the crowd; it was Betz, a bobtailed cat Elder. She spoke aloud what all others were thinking. "How are we to win a battle, let alone a war, without the talon of our feathered brothers and sisters? It will be impossible if the sky is owned by our enemy. We know the Old Poem speaks of the fate of the Oonakestree. If the royal line were ever to fall into the hands of the enemy, all who sprout feathers would put their lives in danger when they were to take flight." She closed her eyes, took a deep breath, and spoke clearly, recalling the Old Poem:

"The sky will stay empty from feather and beak.
While the Oonakestree lies hidden, all will be bleak."

Honu cleared his throat. This silenced and refocused the attention of the beach. "Cat mother, you speak true," he said. "Until we have saved our Oonakestree from this dark destiny and freed him from the Venomous Ones, the feathered are warned by the Old Poem to stay grounded. They are to let no air pass beneath their wings, lest they risk their lives. The Venomous Ones have their flying minions roaming the skies as we gather here now. All of our winged brethren are not to fly but will be escorted home tonight."

Don-Don, a lizard Elder, spoke up loudly. He was jeweled with two thin lines of radiant scales, which started above his shoulders and ran down his sides to his belly. The blue-green scales were interrupted by laces of scars from the ancient battles he had fought in. "Father Honu, we are bound to our king and queen, the Old Poem, and the light. You will have the tail, claw, and jaw of every pure and good lizard that roams the Desert Realm, as bound by my word. We will not rest until the Oonakestree is freed and the Venomous Ones are stopped!"

These passionate words brought the crowd out of their silence and into a loud and lively state.

Honu was pleased to see the passion of the Elders—it would be needed

They all quieted as he spoke again.

"The Old Poem has spoken to me of three who can save the Oonakestree:

The brethren triad, with hearts of gold,
will fight to regain what the evil ones hold.
With tools from the north and a shell from the line,
paths guided and guarded by nature divine."

Lyca, an elk father, spoke up from the gathering. "Honu, do we know who the three are?"

"We believe we do. If the Elders here tonight on the Gathering Beach are in agreement, we will send a spy to confirm that they are the three the poem has foretold."

Without pause, all the Elders cried out in unison, "We accept this!" Their response was so loud, united, and strong that it caused a single ring to rise up and run across the surface of the water.

Honu was pleased at their response and replied, "May the light guide our decisions and illuminate our paths."

Honu looked lovingly at his brothers and sisters of the desert and then turned to make his way back down the rocky path. By the time his foot touched the damp sand of the beach, all the animals were gone. Only a myriad of sandy tracks remained. As he started his way south toward his home, something flew out of the night and hovered over him.

"Am I to go, then, Honu?" the zigzagging, fluttering thing said before it landed on top of his shell.

"Yes, you will fly tonight. They must pass the first test. We must be sure they are indeed the three the Old Poem speaks of." Honu craned his long neck up and around to address his rider. "Your family has been true and loyal in your walk with the light. This journey you are to make tonight is of great importance. Fly safe. If you have trouble convincing them, they will trust the word of their feathered friend, the one who watches over them."

The bat did not reply but flew away to find the three.

Three

The sun slowly crept up from behind the eastern mountains but quickly warmed the cloudless morning sky. Three young hares lay asleep in their underground home, unaware of the night's dire events.

The den was warm and cozy, and although it was nothing more than a nondescript hole in the desert, it was their home—it was where they had been born and grown up. Hints of daylight bounced down the veins of mica that lined the tunnel and kept their home out of total darkness.

Nick, the oldest and the largest of the three brothers, lay sprawled on his side across the back wall of their subterranean home. He was in a deep sleep. Cade, the middle brother, was only a bit smaller than Nick and still had some growing to do. He was also fast asleep, snoring away in a tight ball. Cade was sometimes known to sleepwalk, but he never believed his brothers when they told him the crazy things he said or did. Sam, the youngest, was normally a long, sound sleeper; however, this morning, he was up first. He stood wide eyed and fully awake, looking up into the long tunnel of their den, while small pebbles ran down and bounced off his toes in all directions.

"Someone is coming," he whispered to himself.

The pebbles continued to run out on to the ground, and now a scraping and bumping noise was coming down with them.

"Guys. Guys, someone is coming!" As he uttered the second *guys*, both Nick and Cade were awake and stood on each side of their baby brother, staring up into the shadowy passageway.

Nick spoke calmly. "Be prepared. You know what to do. If it's Eelion or any of his thugs, we have to stun them quickly and escape before they can press the life out of us. They will not take us like they took our parents."

At these words, each of them grabbed a smooth river stone from a pile in the back corner of their den and stretched their arms back, ready to hurl it at the first sight of a forked tongue.

The bumping and scraping slowed down and then stopped altogether. Then a soft squeaking noise came from the tunnel; it was a voice, speaking not in common tongue but in a unique animal language.

Sam took a small step forward and yelled into the hole, "Who are you?"

Nick gently laid his hand on Sam's shoulder. "Sam, hang on. Cade, what is it saying?"

Cade, like their father, Miko, had the gift of the ear, which allowed him to understand and speak the dialect of any animal. He wrinkled his nose and tuned his ears in the direction of the hole. "I think it's safe."

They all lowered their arms but still held on to the stones. Cade tilted his head a bit and let out a few chirps and tweets, which sounded just like the noises they had heard. He said, "You may enter our home."

Again, the pebbles dribbled down. This time, they were followed by a ball of wings that rolled into the middle of the den and stopped with a bump at the feet of the three young hares. The ball unraveled, revealing a small brown bat.

"I am Keoke," he said, now in common tongue. "I come by the request of Honu, the great Elder of the Desert Realm."

"Honu?" Sam asked. "Did you hit your head too hard on the way down? What would Honu want with the three of us?"

"Sam," Nick said, now pulling his brother back by the shoulder, "let him speak."

"Yes, Honu has sent me to you. You three are needed to save the Oonakestree and bring hope to those who walk in the light."

"What in the heck is a Lookakesteree?" Sam said.

"The *Oonakestree*. It is the eagle prince, the unborn leader of the Desert Realm," Keoke replied.

The brothers exchanged puzzled glances as he continued.

"The prince will eventually take the place of his father, King Aridin, as the ruler over the desert sky. But the Venomous Ones have taken the good prince, and they plan to corrupt him by making him one of their own. If they succeed, the entire desert will be under the power of Venom. We will all bow to a Venomous eagle king."

"The Venomous Ones?" Cade asked.

"This is a matter of great importance to all who call the Desert Realm home, young Nick, Cade, and Sam."

Each of them looked surprised, as the bat they had never met called them by name.

"Honu needs to see you, and he will tell you the rest. My job was to confirm that you fulfilled the word of the Old Poem, to confirm that you may indeed be the three written of. And you have confirmed you are worthy of continuing on this important journey."

"What did we confirm?" Cade asked.

Keoke responded, looking directly at Cade. "Actually, it was *you* who confirmed the first test of the Old Poem. It says one of the chosen three will have the gift of the ear. It foretold of you.

"The three will move freely, through all earthen land
with the ear of clarity as part of their clan.
Whether common insect or majestic mare,
all is clear for the ear of this hare."

"While the Oonakestree is held by the Venomous Ones, all birds who take flight put their lives at risk. They have millions of flying warriors now patrolling the skies, and they will be commanded to destroy any feathered animal they see in the air. If they succeed in their plan, all birds will be killed or grounded forever, and the sky will be filled with only flying Venomous bugs." He shook his head.

Sam suddenly spoke up. "Olivia! What about Olivia? Is she OK?"

At that moment, Olivia, a small gray owl with dazzling golden eyes, stepped out from the tunnel and into their home.

"I'm OK, Sam. Thank you. All that Keoke says is true. I am forbidden to fly, as are all birds. I only hope the Oonakestree will be saved from their terrible plans."

All three of them cared for Olivia very much, because she had always shown them great kindness and love, especially when the boys' parents had been taken from them. She lived in an ancient five-armed saguaro that shadowed the entrance to their den in the evenings. She was the closest thing they had to a mother right now.

"Would we be fighting the Venomous Ones?" Sam asked.

"Yes, you will likely fight many on this quest. Some will be ordered to kill you, while others will just hunt you for sport or dinner."

Sam's response was quick and full of passion. "Count me in. Any chance to avenge our parents—count me in!"

"This decision must be one of unity. There is no other way," Keoke warned.

Nick, Cade, and Sam looked at one another and nodded. Then they all turned to Olivia, and her eyes seemed to glow in the dimly lit den.

She nodded back at them and smiled. "You are all so dear to me. May the light grant you favor and guide your every step."

Nick said, "We will do everything we can to save the Oonakestree, the animals of the Desert Realm, and the way of the light."

"This is wonderful news! We must leave now and travel to Honu's lair. I will lead you there."

Cade asked, "Honu's lair? Wow! What do we bring?"

"Your hearts and your courage. All other tools needed will be provided to you. We must travel quickly while there is still confusion in the air. For now, I am able to fly with safe passage, so follow me. Cade, listen for my voice." Keoke turned and clumsily jumped up to the entrance of the tunnel and started to climb his way out.

With sadness in her eyes, Olivia kissed each of them on the cheek. "Thank you for doing this. I love you all. If I could go with you, I would."

They all felt the oncoming rush of tears, but before a single drop could fall on the floor of their den, they shot up the tunnel. Cade was out first; he spotted Keoke and began to follow the fluttering bat. Nick and Sam quickly caught up with him and joined the chase across the desert.

By the time Olivia made her way out of the den, her dear friends were already hidden by the terrain. She could see only a faint glimpse of Keoke flying in the distance. Olivia walked back over to her cactus home, stopped, and looked around. When all seemed clear, she leaped up and fluttered her wings several times, lifting herself up toward the hole in the towering plant. She landed in the opening of her burrowed abode and then turned back around to see if she could spot the boys from the higher elevation. She was met by a large black-and-yellow insect face that hung upside down from the top of her home's entrance.

"Hello, beautiful. That sure was a close call. I could have sworn I saw you flying." The voice was that of Bazzering, a large, cruel wasp that had risen quickly in the ranks of the Venomous Ones following his conversion.

"Luckily, you are safely tucked away in your home. Do you know what happens to little birdies that fly right now? Do you, little one?" As he said this, his black forked tongue appeared and ran along the left edge of his face. She could see herself in his cold, black-mirrored eyes.

"Well, do you know?"

She was scared but spoke with strength and courage as she looked into his emotionless face. "Yes, the Venomous Ones are rulers of the sky…for now. You have kidnapped the Oonakestree."

"Yes, you are correct. So it looks like you will be home for a while." Bazzering laughed, and five more giant yellow wasp heads appeared around the entrance of Olivia's home. "Home is where the heart is. Ha, ha, ha." Bazzering's laugh was cold and uncaring. With his final *ha*, he and his minions flew off into the morning sky.

Four

Although Keoke was a bit clumsy going up and down a sandy sloping tunnel, he fluttered with silent grace and speed through the air. The hares had followed his zigzagging flight since the morning. The terrain had now shifted from sandy cacti-covered desert to rocky brush-covered hills. The boys were near exhaustion; they had stopped only once for water and a bit of prickly pear.

Keoke stopped his flight and perched on a long, smooth branch of a magnificent green tree whose twisting branches splintered up into the evening sky. It stood alone in the middle of the steep and narrow ravine, and it was almost as broad as the canyon itself. Water-worn stones of all sizes were scattered everywhere. Heavy monsoon rains had recently pushed through this part of the desert, as small, still pools of rainwater reflected the light of the stars.

"We are here. I must go." Keoke smiled at them. "Listen to Honu."

Before the brothers could say anything, he was gone into the night. They wished they had been able to thank him for his guidance and hoped they would see him again.

Sam whispered, "Do you see anything? If he's almost eight hundred years old, he must be gigantic."

A soft but strong voice materialized from what the boys had casually seen as a large shadowed boulder. "I am here, and I am strengthened by seeing you here."

The boys turned around and, without a thought, bowed to the great tortoise. This was no legend; he was real, and he was magnificent. Sam was right: Honu was gigantic and by far the biggest tortoise any of them had ever seen. If they were to stand on one another's shoulders, they might reach the top of Honu's shell. He was great, indeed.

Honu's blue eyes seemed to glow in the moonlight as he spoke to them. "Follow me."

Their ears suddenly turned upward at an oncoming buzzing sound. The three of them ducked down as a large swarm twisted through the air over them.

"They saw us," Sam whispered to Honu.

"Yes, Sam. But what did they see? They are trained to seek and destroy birds in flight, not hares or tortoises." He stopped. "At least not yet. This is why *the three* are said to be hares. Your kind is found in every realm across the earth. And like tortoises, hares are nothing to cause alarm." Honu shot them a quick wink as he said this.

"Thank you, Honu," Sam said, and his ears relaxed.

They followed him under the umbrella of the green giant, leaving tracks through the layer of tiny yellow flowers recently shed by the tree. The moonlight lit up a large jagged opening in the canyon wall. If asked, each would have sworn he hadn't seen it when they had first arrived and looked around. Honu stepped into the opening. A soft white light rose up around him from the clear crystals that lined the wall. It followed him along as he continued deeper into the formation.

"You have been told of the kidnapping of the prince. If he is not rescued, the Venomous Ones will usher in a cold and cruel time. It will change the balance of life in our realm and possibly beyond to others. The Old Poem has spoken of three brothers who possess special gifts that can save the innocent from this horrible future."

Nick said, "Honu, if you think we are the chosen ones, we will serve you and the way of the light."

Cade added, "Just tell us what we need to do."

Honu bowed his head down to them and spoke earnestly. "This task will be filled with danger. Venom beasts of all kinds will be commanded to hunt you. This is why you will be armed." Honu turned his head toward the back of his cave. "There are your weapons."

Resting against the wall were three long reeds, a mound of smooth round stones, and a large pile of cactus spines. Next to them were three white woven bags; the material was smooth and glowed in the light from the crystals.

Cade bent down, picked up a reed, and inspected it. "Honu, how are these sticks…actually, how are these reeds going to help us?"

"Tonight, I will teach you how to make the most of your new tools. They will enable you and protect you."

The reeds that Honu had for them were not a common reed found on any riverbank but rather a rare variety that grew only in the frozen ponds on Mount Cavas. They had been harvested by beavers that journeyed up the mountains to work in the icy waters. The reeds were then dried and delivered to gypsy caterpillars, who spun a fine silk across their surface. After the silk hardened, the reeds were brought to the Desert Realm to cactus-dwelling birds that cured them with daily treatments of cactus flesh. This ancient process made the reeds virtually unbreakable.

"These reeds are light but are as hard as stone. You will be glad for them, but remember, they are weapons *and* tools. The bags have been woven for you and will fit upon your backs. They will store food and weapons and will help you to carry something of great importance to me." He backed away, and behind him on the ground was a small tortoise shell. It looked exactly like Honu's but was only a fraction of the size.

"This shell belonged to my son, Zona. His life was taken by the Venomous Ones during the early days of their uprising." Honu closed his eyes. "He would have been almost three hundred years old now. It warms my heart to know that although he has risen to the light, he can still be a part of the fight against the Venomous Ones and help stop their evil plans."

They stepped toward Zona's shell, and each of them placed a paw on top of it.

"You will take his shell with you on your quest; it will provide you and the Oonakestree much-needed protection from our enemies."

Honu spent the rest of the night in the soft glow of his den telling them about ancient times and teaching them how to use their new tools.

Five

D anix, a dull-yellow and partly translucent scorpion, clicked his curved pincers and blinked all six of his eyes in excitement. He was always nervous before he delivered a field update to his lord and master, the ancient lizard Hillmaken. He was one of the largest lizards in the Desert Realm; his love and dedication to the Venom Stone and its powers had changed him. He hardly resembled the young agile lizard he had once been; now his legs, body, and tail were rugged and powerful.

"The final pieces are in place, sir. Eelion has taken and secured the Oonakestree, and the unborn prince is hidden safely away, awaiting his fate. Shall I send word to begin the second phase of our operation?" His legs jittered anxiously as he awaited Hillmaken's answer.

Crystals were known to possess the ability to absorb and emit the energy of the beings around them. The crystal veins that lined Hillmaken's underground lair slowly pulsated with a deep, angry red glow.

"My legions are prepared for their final march to rid the desert of the cowards who have rejected the power of

Venom. Our spies tell us they are looking for three they say the Old Poem tells of, three who can rescue the unborn prince. Whoever *they* are, they will never find or rescue the Oonakestree. He is mine."

Danix cowered as Hillmaken stomped around his nest. Blobs of green poison sprayed from the lizard's mouth as he continued his rant. "The new prince will soon have venom coursing through his veins, and his conversion will shift control of the skies to us. The feathered will have to accept him; they will have *no* choice."

Hillmaken let out a horrible hissing laugh, which caused Danix to shrink toward the closest wall. His plans were coming together just as he had calculated. But he not only wanted victory over those he saw as his enemies; he also yearned for their complete destruction. Many years ago, Hillmaken had played a sinister role in the events that led to the start of the Venom Wars. In his mind, that war had never ended, despite the meaningless truce, but had only ebbed and flowed over time.

"Danix, find a bat!"

The scorpion crawled away from the safety of the wall and then stood at full attention in front of his leader. His claws still snapped nervously.

"Send word to Honu that I am willing to make a *new* truce with him—a final and lasting peace accord for the Desert Realm. Tell him I will bring the Oonakestree to the Gathering Beach the morning of the full moon. Tell him that *all* of the Edlers must be there to make the new truce legitimate and binding."

Michael C. Baumann

A thick strand of green-yellow drool plopped to the ground as spoke. "And send word to Bazzering that I want an update on the progress of our recruits."

Danix blinked his dark, cold eyes and darted out of a small opening, leaving his master alone in his lair.

Six

"You have listened and learned well and have a good sense of your tools. Now, one more thing: I need each of you to take out your reeds and form into a triangle."

They gathered together as he had instructed, each placing his reed on the shoulder of the brother to his right.

"You must keep this stone within your triangle. Use only your reeds."

Honu kicked a small stone toward them. It zipped through the air. Sam brought his reed up and stopped the rock with a sharp cracking sound. He looked down at the stone and then back up at his brothers. He held in his giggle as he swung. "Keep this in the triangle, guys."

The jagged stone skipped across the ground toward Nick, who dropped his reed straight down and blocked it. He swung down and hit it toward Cade, who leaned right and hit the stone right back to him. They continued to swat the stone across their triangle, where it skipped and skimmed along the desert floor. Sand and pebbles jumped as the rock etched its way across the ground. The stone bounced so fast off their reeds that it was merely a blur in the dust.

"Stop now, young hares."

Cade stooped and snagged the stone out of the air with his paw, and they all looked back at Honu.

"Your time with me is done for now. Your journey is underway, and your destination is below you."

They looked down in amazement. The ground was no longer a smooth desert floor.

"It's a map!" Nick exclaimed.

The skimming and skipping of the stone had carved out a detailed map that showed the Desert Realm in its entirety, from the Dune Plains in the west to the Cacti Canyons in the east.

Cade added, "Amazing!"

Honu replied, "Yes, it is a map. And you *are* the three the Old Poem has spoken of.

"With reeds of stone and hearts of gold,
mapped in the earth, secret paths will unfold."

Sam spoke up as he pointed down. "Look! The map—it's moving."

Cade and Nick leaned in and saw a small eddy that was circling in the sand. According to the map, it appeared to be in the Calaas Mountains.

"That is where you will start your search for the Oonakestree." Honu felt hope rise in him, for he knew they were indeed the ones the Old Poem told of. There was now a way to stop the desert from falling. "The map you created will guide you. The Pathway Stone that Cade holds will work for you only once each day."

The boys still stood examining the detailed map at their feet as Honu continued.

"Now it is time for you to leave. You will have friends along your way who will help you with your search. Go now, and may the light guide you safely." Honu turned and disappeared into his lair and was instantly gone.

They said nothing as they stowed the stones and spines into their new packs. Nick and Cade slid each of their reeds through the leg openings of Zona's shell. Then they squatted on either side of it, and Sam secured the reeds through loops on the tops and bottoms of their packs. They stood up and carried the shell out of Honu's lair.

Once outside, Nick scanned the night sky, pointed, and said, "We can follow the North Star for now. That should lead us to the Calaas Mountains. We can use the Pathway Stone in the morning. Let's go."

Seven

The sun rose quickly out of the horizon, and in an instant, the red glow of first light was replaced by a bright-blue morning. All was clear except for rows of soft brush-stroked clouds that lined the western sky. A bird-seeking swarm passed over the three trekking hares but paid them no mind.

Sam had been leading his shell-toting brothers since they had left Honu's lair, keeping his ears and eyes on alert as they had been instructed. So far their quest had been remarkably quiet, but it had been a bit unsettling not seeing or hearing any birds in the sky. There were no doves cooing and no owls hooting; instead, there were only insects flying about. It was like nothing they had ever seen: swarms rolled in buzzing waves all over the sky.

"Sun is up. We might as well stop and eat," Sam said.

The idea of a rest sounded good to all of them. The new day meant they could again use the Pathway Stone to refine and refocus their path.

Nick spoke up. "I'll go find some food. I see some big barrels over there. Stay here."

Cade and Sam did not object. They had already taken off their packs and had plopped down in the rocky sand.

"I hope he brings back all of them," Cade said.

The monsoon season had delivered more rain than usual, which meant the cacti would be full of fresh, plump fruit. The flesh of the barrel fruit would provide water and nourishment for the trio, and they could save its tiny black seeds as snacks for later. The round, squat cacti grew together in clustered bunches.

They watched Nick as he hopped over to a patch where three large barrels grew together; the largest had almost a dozen large fruit spread across its crown. The sweet yellow treats looked like shrunken pineapples now that their flowers had dried up. Nick lifted up his reed, got up on tiptoes, and forced the end of it under the base of a fruit. He was careful not to touch the razor-sharp red spines that protected the cactus from top to bottom. He pulled down on the reed, and with little of Nick's effort, the miniature pineapple popped straight up and then bounced off the spines and fell to the ground. Nick smiled, and his stomach growled. He hopped a step to the right and began to pry out the next fruit. Directly behind him, a webby door silently opened up from out of the desert, and four hairy brown legs emerged. Nick heard nothing as he repositioned his reed on the cacti and pulled down.

A large brown spider with two rows of cold black eyes was now out from the ground and was crouching in his shadow. Nick was surprised at how difficult this second fruit was compared to the first. As he pulled down at a slightly different angle, he unknowingly inched closer to the spider. It was almost half his size, and Nick was no small hare. The sandy door popped open again, and four more hairy legs sprang out, followed by another set of cold eyes. Quickly and silently, the second spider was out, and it too sat silently in Nick's shadow.

He pulled down on his reed, almost hanging from it until the yellow fruit popped free. Just as it hit the ground, the eight-legged assassins made their move toward him, unleashing shrill hisses as they sprang. Nick whirled around to see two Venom spiders leaping at him.

Cade and Sam had loaded their reeds with cactus spines as they sprinted toward Nick. The duo drew in deep breaths and fired at the attackers. Cade's first shot was true; his spine exploded into an eye of the first spider, sending it tumbling backward with a gurgling hiss. Its four front legs frantically

struggled, trying to pull out the spine buried in the top of its head.

Nick brought his reed up to protect himself from the second spider just as two more spines came whistling in. One blew clean through the creature's bulbous abdomen, while the other pierced its head, just under its first row of eyes. The spines killed it before it could finish its attack. Nick turned to see Cade and Sam running toward him, each with a reed in hand.

"You guys saved my life!" Nick panted, truly thankful to be alive.

They each gathered up more fruit then made their way back toward Zona's shell. It was a relief to put some distance between themselves and the spiders, one of which was still struggling to remove the spine; however, now only two arms kept up the search.

"Let's eat!" Sam suggested as he sat down next to his pack.

They each grabbed one of the little yellow gems, tore off the dried crown, and bit into the soft, sweet flesh of the fruit. They nibbled around the pocket of seeds that grew clumped together inside. They each ate two fruit and immediately felt better.

Nick wiped juice from his chin and said, "We need to get moving." He wiped again with his other paw and continued, "New day, new map!"

Cade reached into a hidden fold of his pack and pulled out the Pathway Stone. They formed up again, just as Honu had instructed them, and shot the Pathway Stone back and forth across their triangle. Their reeds echoed with woody pops each time one connected with the stone, which moved so fast it could hardly be seen amid the sand, pebbles, and rocks that sprayed in all directions. Out of the dust, another map began to appear at their feet; this time, it was an image of a mountain range, with a single peak that was dramatically higher than the rest. The map had remarkable detail, showing rocks, trees, and a river that ran near the mountain range.

"Look!" Nick said as he pointed to the etching.

Cade snatched the rock out of the air with his left paw and tucked it back into his pack. They all leaned in and inspected the new image. Atop the tallest mountain, there was movement: it was another tiny eddy of sand.

"Is that Mount Flagg?" Sam asked as he stood up and scratched behind his ear.

Cade responded, "Yes, that's the Calaas Range, and Mount Flagg seems to be alive."

Nick added, "And it looks like we need to go to the top."

They all turned and looked north toward the giant snow-covered mountains, which were just half a day's run away.

"Why would the Venomous Ones put the Oonakestree up there? They usually stay away from anything cold. It slows 'em down too much," Sam said.

"It may not make sense, but Honu said we need to follow the Pathway Stone. So let's get moving," Nick said, still looking down in amazement at the detail of the map.

Soon they were back in their traveling formation: Cade and Nick carried Zona's shell between them, while Sam led the way. The trio's pace was quick and steady as they made their way across the rolling desert toward the snowy mountains in the distance.

"We are far from home now," Sam said. "I hope Olivia is OK."

They all missed her. She was more than a friend to them; she was their family. She had been there the day Eelion and his henchmen attacked and killed the boys' parents. During the mayhem, Olivia had flown each of the young hares safely up inside her cactus home, away from the violent horde of snakes, toads, and frogs. She had promised them that night that she would always protect them. Every night since then, she had circled over them as they foraged in the desert, keeping an eye out for danger. They all wished that she was soaring above them now.

They had traveled far that day; their desert was now far behind them. The air was cooler and the terrain had become rugged and rocky, with no signs of cacti. As they crested a brush-covered knoll, Mount Flagg came into full view. They stopped and looked up in awe. The towering peak was hidden in thick gray clouds that swirled around it.

"Do you hear that?" Cade asked.

"Yes, it's the river ahead," Nick responded. "It sounds fast."

"No, not the river. Look behind us!" Cade cried.

Sam and Nick turned to see something large and gray running toward them. It yelped and howled as it raced over the hills.

"It's a coyote. Run!" Sam yelled.

This coyote had been chasing after their scent since they had left Honu's. It was not a common scavenging coyote that the boys had seen growing up in the desert; this one had Venom running through its veins. It was Eelion's and Hillmaken's first successful mammal convert; they had classified their new species as simply a *yote* and renamed him Ilioino. He had once been a well-respected pack leader, but Hillmaken had tricked him into his conversion. Now he was one of the hundreds the yotes that now mindlessly served the Venomous Ones. He was easily double the size of any unconverted coyote. He now had very little hair—only sporadic splotches of matted fur that clung from his lumpy gray hide. His skin looked dead. His long purple tongue flopped about, and yellow foam flew from the edges of his jowls as he sprinted toward them.

"It's coming. Hurry!" Sam shouted.

As they sprinted toward the fast-flowing river, their footing went bad as the firm earth turned into loose river rock.

"Get ready for me, guys!" Sam yelled as he pulled his reed free from his pack. He sprinted ahead of them and lowered it down until it caught the edge of a large flat stone. The reed bowed but did not break, propelling him straight up into the air. He flipped completely over and landed on top of Zona's shell. He turned around to check on their pursuer and came face to face with a snapping set of jaws that clipped off several of his whiskers. Ilioino stumbled but quickly regained his pursuit and lunged again. Sam swung his reed. It connected into the animal's lower jaw with a wet crack. Ilioino tumbled and tripped over himself, yelping as he bounced across the smooth rocks. The blow slowed him, but it did not deter him. He quickly regained his sprint and again closed in on them.

Sam kept his balance atop the shell as Nick and Cade sprinted toward the river. He reached into a fold of one of the straps on his pack and pulled out three long, sharp spines. He loaded them all into the end of the reed, one after the other. He drew in a deep breath and fired them at Ilioino. The spines found their target as all three landed in the yote's snout. One sailed directly into his left nostril. However, the spines had little effect, and he continued to chase after them. Cade and Nick zigged and zagged but were not able to shake him. Now the river was upon them, and there was nowhere else to go.

"Head toward that rock!" Cade yelled and signaled with a nod.

Sam almost fell off as his brothers cut left and began to run along the waterline toward an enormous stone ramp that jutted out over the river. Sam regained his balance, and Ilioino leaped again. Sam swung, and his reed smashed squarely into the crazed yote's snout, knocking out most of the teeth in its lower jaw. The blow momentarily stunned him, but he got back up and shook away the pain and continued after them.

Sam squatted down, leaning over the front of the shell, his head between his brothers, and yelled, "What are you doing? I can't swim!"

"Hang on to the shell, Sam. It's our only chance," Nick yelled back. He now saw what Cade had in mind.

They cut hard right and started up the long overhanging rock. Ilioino faltered trying to make the turn but quickly regained his footing and scrambled up the incline. The turn broke Sam's grip, and he tumbled off the top of his ride. He was sliding off the shell but stopped himself by shooting his legs apart, landing each one on each of the shell-supporting reeds.

"Sam!" Cade grunted as his brother's weight pushed down on him.

Sam scrambled back on top of the shell in time to see the end of the rock disappear. Nick and Cade jumped out over the river. Sam held on to the shell and continued to swing his reed at Ilioino, who had leaped out after them. They all splashed into the river. After several seconds of swirling underwater chaos, Zona's shell popped up to the surface. Nick and Cade were still secured to it but were now on their backs. Sam held on to the shell as he burst up out of the water, pulling in a deep breath. With one paw still holding his reed, he climbed out of water onto the bottom of the floating shell. He looked down at his brothers.

"Are you two OK?"

Cade and Nick nodded just as a gurgling growl exploded out of the river behind them, and the snake-eyed coyote with missing teeth began to paddle toward them.

"Kick, you guys!" Sam yelled.

Nick and Cade frantically paddled their long webbed feet against the flow of the river. Their effort began to create space between them and Ilioino.

"It's working. Keep kicking, Cade," Nick shouted.

Nick and Cade continued to flutter their feet, which held them steady against the flow of the river. Ilioino soon gave up his fight against the current, stopped paddling, and disappeared downstream.

"Can you guys get us to the shore?" Sam asked.

They kicked, and Sam used his reed to change their direction. The shell moved across the river with ease, landing them on the rocky shore on the other side of the river. Sam jumped down and untied the reeds from Nick and Cade's packs, who rolled away from the shell onto the rocky shore in exhaustion.

Eight

"Honu? Honu, are you here?"

The messenger bat looked around nervously as it sat perched on a small branch of the giant green tree that grew near Honu's lair. Its eyes shifted about, and its ears were on alert as it scanned around for the great tortoise. Without movement or sound, Honu appeared near the base of the tree, looking up at the bat.

"Yes, my winged brother," Honu quietly said.

"Honu, I deliver a message from Hillmaken, who requires the company of you and the Elders at the Gathering Beach, on the morning of the full moon. He will negotiate a new and lasting peace in exchange for the Oonakestree."

Honu and Hillmaken had history together. They had known each other before the Venom had infected and corrupted the great lizard's mind. Although Honu had hoped that his old friend would give up his dedication to the Venom Stone, he feared that it had been far too long, and its horrible poison was now part of the fabric that made him.

Honu knew that Hillmaken could not be trusted. However, he saw little choice but to take his proposal. "On behalf of King Aridin, tell Hillmaken that I accept his offer. The Elders of the Desert Realm will negotiate a new peace in exchange for the Oonakestree."

Without a response, the bat flew away.

As Honu stood quietly thinking of what was to come, he whispered words of the Old Poem.

"Poison and purity—a colossal divide.
Each committed to the way of its side.
Poison infects, corrupts, and corrodes
the once-peaceful nights of innocent homes.
Venom versus light.
Wrong versus right."

Nine

Mountains were the one place the Venomous Ones had a difficult time seeding and propagating their way, due mainly to the cold climate. Most creatures that had accepted the path of Venom were generally reptiles, amphibians, or insects, none of whom appreciated a fresh layer of fallen snow. Hillmaken had made great efforts to recruit and convert the animals that lived in the higher altitudes, but most had declined his offer.

The sound of the rushing river filled the hares' ears as they lay on the rocky shore. The brilliant sun and dry air quickly dried their brown-gray coats. Their escape from Ilioino had brought them safely to the base of the Calaas Mountains.

"Well, that's one way to get across the river," Nick said as he pulled his reed out of the shell.

"Yes, and a good way for Sam to learn to swim." Cade laughed.

Sam ignored the comment. "Was that coyote really Venomous? I've never seen anything like that. Its eyes…they looked like snake eyes."

"Yes, it was one of the Venomous Ones," Nick confirmed as he and Cade flipped Zona's shell over right side up.

"Really—a coyote? I thought only insects and scaled creatures accepted the way of Venom," Sam remarked.

"Honu said their goal is to make *every* creature follow in the way of Venom. I think that coyote took them up on that offer."

"I hope we never see it again," Sam quietly said as he rearranged the cactus spines in his pack.

Cade walked over and put his hand on his little brother's back. "You know you saved us, Sam. If you hadn't fought it off, we would have been his lunch."

Sam smiled at the rare brotherly compliment.

"OK, let's eat and then start heading up to Mount Flagg," Nick said.

The barrel fruit they had gathered had somehow remained unharmed in their packs. They sat in the sun enjoying the sweet fruit, watching the river run past them.

"We have to go to the top, huh?" Cade asked.

"That is what the map showed," Nick said.

"Let's go, then," Sam said.

They stowed away the last remaining barrel fruits into their packs and donned them. Nick and Cade again slid their reeds through the shell, and Sam helped secure them to their packs.

Nick gazed up at the towering peak. "Let's get into the mountain and find a place to rest before the sun goes down. We all need it."

Suddenly, their ears perked up and turned downriver toward a buzzing that was coming their way. Sam stood and grabbed his reed and was ready to swing at whatever it was. The flying thing stopped and landed on a branch of a dead tree on the riverbank. To their relief and surprise, it was not an insect but rather a hummingbird.

The bird greeted them. "Hello, brothers."

Brilliant-green plumage covered his back and wings, while radiant purple feathers lined its head and neck. His chest was white.

"Who are you?" Cade asked.

"I am Avery. Honu sent me to make sure you are still safe on your path and to deliver a message."

"Hey, how come you can fly? I thought all birds weren't allowed to right now. Couldn't you be killed?" Sam asked.

"You're right, Sam. However, the drones that are seeking out birds often overlook my kind because we are small and sound like their swarms in flight. The Venomous Ones aren't always the smartest of creatures. Poison in your blood will do that to you." Avery joked.

"What's the message?" Nick asked.

"Last night, after meditating on the Old Poem, Honu had a dream—one that said that you, Nick, must take the Balancing Stone that rests on Mount Flagg. It is critical to your mission."

"What is the Balancing Stone?" Nick asked.

"You can see it from here," Avery quickly responded. "Look up the mountain. See? It is on that ledge on the west side."

Cade spoke up. "What stone? The only thing on the west side of the mountain is that huge boulder, not a stone. You can't mean that."

"That was what Honu told me. He said that the Old Poem showed him in his dream. Nick, you must find a way to take it with you."

They all looked up at the mammoth boulder; it was easily seen from the banks of the river. It was dark gray with thin white veins of crystal and mica splintering across its surface. It rested on the wide ledge. Balancing on its tapered point, it seemed to defy gravity.

"How am I supposed to take that with me? It's impossible! There isn't an animal anywhere that could move that, let alone take it."

Avery looked at them, tilted his head, chirped several times, and then flew away.

"What did he say, Cade?" Nick asked.

Cade looked up at the great stone on the mountain and said, "It is from the Old Poem:

"Faith from the brothers, who trek far from their homes,
provides strength to secure the greatest of stones."

"It must mean something else. We will be up there in the morning—we'll see then," Nick said, still doubting the hummingbird's message.

The sun slowly disappeared as they made their way up into the tall, cool pines of Mount Flagg. They stopped to make camp just below the start of the snow line. Hares were amazing diggers. Within minutes, the trio had burrowed out a remarkably large shelter near the base of a towering pine. Zona's shell was hidden with them as they huddled together for warmth. They fell asleep quickly and slept soundly that night.

Ten

The bat delivered Honu's response to Hillmaken and then fluttered back up into the night sky.

"Excellent! Those deniers and rejecters will finally accept the way of Venom or die." Hillmaken was all too pleased that his plans were coming together. "I will finish what I should have long ago. I will finally bring a new and *better* life to the Desert Realm—a life where Venom gives power and strength to those who accept it."

Hillmaken's lair was not a pleasant place to visit; it reeked of death and was littered with the skeletons of various creatures he had devoured, all of which were missing the skull. Hillmaken's rage and short temper had driven him to even devour other lizards on occasion. Stories and rumors had spread across the realm that even his own son had not escaped the wrath of his father.

"Danix, Danix!" Hillmaken bellowed.

His loyal scorpion lieutenant popped out from one of the many small tunnels that led to Hillmaken's lair.

"Yes, my lord," Danix responded nervously.

"What news have you heard? How are my armies?"

"All is going as planned, Hillmaken, sir. Bazzering says they are being converted as fast as they can. He hopes to have all of them ready by the full moon."

"Hope? Hope?" He stomped as he spoke. "Followers of the Venom do not rely on hope. Hope is for the weak. All of them *will* be armed and ready for battle. Is that clear?"

The crystals in his lair pulsed with a deep-red glow as Hillmaken ranted and raged in circles around his home.

"Yes, sir, your commands are clear. However, he said it is just taking longer than we had anticipated. Many of the flyers are dying from the direct exposure to the stone. It is very strong." Danix cringed, expecting a blow from Hillmaken's tail, which often followed an ill-received message.

"Inform Bazzering that his flyers *will* be ready by the full moon, and he should be prepared for a visit from me to inspect his progress. I do not want to hear any more talk of *hope*. Understood?"

"Yes, my lord." Danix quickly left the lair, thankful to leave without a beating.

Eleven

While they slept in their newly dug den, more thick gray clouds had rolled in and frosted the mountains with a blanket of fresh snow. A wall of snow stacked up and covered the entrance of their overnight accommodations. Although birds were forbidden to fly, this did not keep them from singing today. A chorus of sweet songs echoed through the forest and gently roused the trio from their sleep. Sam woke up first and broke through the snowy door, stepping out into the forest.

"Whoa!" he said.

As he made his way into the morning light, Sam saw pure-white forest in every direction. He looked down and realized something else had changed: instead of seeing the normal brown-gray fur covering his body, his entire coat had turned white.

"You guys! You gotta come up here!"

Cade and Nick awoke and stepped out into the morning sun. To Sam's surprise, their coats had also changed.

"Sam, you're all white," Cade exclaimed as he pointed at him.

"So are you, Cade," Nick said, laughing. "Amazing!"

"Let's get the Pathway Stone out so we can get moving," Sam suggested.

They stepped back into their makeshift den, formed into their triangle, and began to shoot the Pathway Stone back and forth among them. Snow, soil, and stones sprayed around as they bounced the stone back and forth to one another. The cracking and popping of the reeds echoed across the mountain like a chorus of working woodpeckers. Nick nodded, and Cade snatched the stone out of the air. Another map appeared at their feet. Mount Flagg was carved out in detail, and there was a twisting line that marked their path up the mountain, leading to another swirling eddy of soil.

"I guess you really are meant to get the Balancing Stone," Cade said. "The map shows a path that goes right by it on our way to the top."

"I still think it means something else. That stone is a mountain itself. There is no way I can carry that. It must be a riddle or a clue," Nick surmised.

The three now-white hares again packed up their gear, secured the shell, and began the climb further up into the mountain. They hiked for several hours, following the path the stone had mapped for them, when they came upon the Balancing Stone. Its name was apt, for the mammoth boulder sat on a rocky ledge, seeming to balance on a tapered point. It was taller than many of the pine trees that grew from the steep, snowy cliffs.

"Come on, Nick. Pick that thing up so we can get going," Cade urged, nudging Sam.

"Guys, I am telling you: it's impossible. There must be another meaning. Honu's dream might be speaking in a riddle. Another test, maybe?" Nick was not too happy with his brother's comments.

"I don't think so. You just need to grab that thing so we can move on." Sam laughed, seeing Nick's improbable task. "You're the oldest. You can do it."

Nick did not want to hear any more of his brother's ribbing, so he decided to at least go check it out. Perhaps there was something near it or on it that would be of importance. Sam and Cade stayed back with the shell as Nick hopped out onto the rocky shelf. As he came closer, the towering boulder became even more daunting.

"Hurry up, strong guy. Let's go." Sam again laughed.

Nick turned and gave them the same "be quiet" look that their mother had often given them when they would all get spun up and out of control, as brothers often did.

"Well, do you see anything?" Cade yelled.

"I don't think it will fit into your pack, anyway," Sam added with another giggle.

Nick circled around the base of the Balancing Stone, looking for something that would perhaps make sense of Honu's strange request. As he investigated, the jokes from his brothers continued.

"Guys, enough! He couldn't have meant that I actually have to *take* this. It means something else."

Cade and Sam tried to hold in their laughs.

"Fine. I will pick it up!" And with a gesture meant to shut his brothers up, he wrapped his arms as far around the tapered base of the rock as he could, squatted, and lifted.

Cade and Sam stopped their ribbing and stood in awe as cold air kicked up and swirled the fresh snow all around them. The entire mountain started to tremble. Nick actually began to lift the Balancing Stone up off the rocky ledge, and at the same time it began to shrink. In a flash, the once-huge boulder was now a mere rock, roughly the size of the Pathway Stone, and was sitting neatly in Nick's paw. It still stood upright as he held it, just as it had on the ledge.

In unison, Sam and Cade exclaimed, "Cool!"

Nick smiled but did not look up at them. He continued to stare at the Balancing Stone. "Amazing!" Nick said, still in disbelief at what had happened. As Cade and Sam walked out across the ledge to him, he extended his paw and showed them the stone.

Twelve

They had not been gone long, but Olivia missed them terribly. However, something inside her told her that they would find a way to succeed in their dangerous mission. She jumped up to the perch of the opening of her home and looked out into the sky. The blistering sun fought to keep away the threatening clouds that were approaching from the south. She heard a rustling below her and looked down to see a family of quail rambling out of some scrub bush that grew next to the entrance to the boys' home. There were six of them, and they all looked up at her.

The largest one asked, "Olivia?"

"Yes. Who are you?"

"I am Whitt, and these are my children. We need to talk to you; we have heard news of your friends."

"You need to be careful, Whitt. Don't you know what is going on? The Venomous Ones have swarms that are roaming about looking for feathered creatures to kill."

"We are aware that it is not safe to fly. However, we can safely *walk* everywhere. Hillmaken's mindless drones only

know to attack birds in flight, because their transformed brains can focus on only one task at a time. A walking bird is something they cannot comprehend." He winked at her.

"You have news on Nick, Cade, and Sam—are they OK?"

"Word has spread that they are making progress in their trek, but danger surrounds them. Their journey has taken them to the Calaas Mountains." Whitt paused and surveyed the sky. "Come down while none of those flying idiots are about. We need to talk of the plans that are being made."

Olivia confirmed it was clear with another quick scan, and then she leaned forward, opened her wings, and spiraled down to the quail family in several tight loops.

"Children, make her one of us. We still do not want to bring any attention to ourselves."

With their father's word, the quail chicks quickly huddled around Olivia and began to peck at the ground and circle about her in a dusty commotion. When the feathered frenzy stopped, Olivia's appearance had changed. Her light-gray feathers were now covered with smartly placed desert silt and sand, which made her look like a quail. They even fashioned a small twig atop her head, which looked remarkably like the feather plume that sprouted from Whitt's head.

"If we are to help in the cause, we must leave now," Whitt said.

"I am ready."

Whitt's chicks followed him as he started up a small hill that led northwest toward the Great Lake. Olivia the owl-quail followed them.

Thirteen

Nick tucked the Balancing Stone into a fold in his pack and turned his gaze up toward the steep snowy peaks of Mount Flagg. He enjoyed the quiet now that his brothers had stopped their giggling.

"*Now* we can go to the top."

Cade looked upward. "Yeah, but what are we looking for once we get there? The stone showed our path ends at the top, but then what?"

Nick agreed. "I'm not sure, but there is only one way to find out."

"Uh-oh." Sam's ears swiveled as he said this.

Sam peered over the edge of their rocky perch, looking down toward the base of the mountain, toward the river, which could still be faintly heard.

"Do you guys remember that poisonous coyote? Well, he's back."

Nick and Cade joined him and looked down to see Ilioino hobbling up along the rocky bank toward the base of the mountain. From where they looked down, he appeared quite small.

Cade turned to look back up toward the peak of Mount Flagg. "Forget him for now. Let's just get moving. If we get to the top, we'll be ready for him. Together, the three of us can defeat him."

Nick stood and replied to Cade. "Yes, let's—"

"Uh-oh," Sam said once more as he continued to stare down the mountain.

Cade and Nick again leaned back over the edge and saw that several dozen grayish spots had joined Ilioino. The pack of yotes circled around their leader, and they all began to howl. Ilioino joined their chorus and then broke from the circle and ran across onto the low slope of the mountain's base.

Without another word, Nick and Cade secured Zona's shell to their backs, and Sam led the way up the tree-filled slopes of Mount Flagg.

Fourteen

Honu's mind raced as he hiked across the desert; the attack and kidnapping weighed heavily on him. His steady, unyielding pace brought him to the rolling plains of the Red Desert, to Aridin's home. He looked upward as the new-morning light cast a shadow on the rocky entrance to the royal lair. He continued his way around the base of the mesa toward two lonely bean-bearing mesquite trees and then stopped. He whispered something to himself and then approached a large red stone, which was close to twice his size. He placed his head against the stone and pushed. As it rolled away, a rush of hot air whistled out of a concealed passageway. Honu stepped inside and followed its twisting path up into the belly of the mesa. Glowing crystals accompanied him on his way upward. After several steep inclines and a long series of tight switchbacks, Honu saw a hint of natural light ahead of him.

"Aridin?"

"Come in, Honu," a tired voice replied from within.

Honu entered the royal abode and saw Aridin, who did not turn but kept his eyes locked on Sparra. She was resting in the same nest that had recently held the Oonakestree. Two large horned owls with radiant orange eyes stood on either side of the ailing queen. Her husband stood over her as she quietly fought for her life.

Honu was gripped with sorrow as he looked at his old friends, but his voice did not falter as he spoke. "It is good to see you, Aridin."

"Dear brother, I am not sure if it *is* good to see me. I have lost my son. And now maybe my wife…"

Aridin turned toward him, and Honu saw the small bone jutting out of his side.

"Eelion and his henchmen ambushed us—in our home, Honu! Where is the honor in that? They steal my unborn child. They poison my wife." He faced Honu. "And I am not sure she will make it."

Honu stepped next to the nest and assured his friend, "She will survive."

He made a soft clicking noise toward the opening of the tunnel. With a responding click, a small green lizard appeared out of the darkness; it held a single flower in its mouth. Three orange arms sprouted from the middle of the flower's thin red petals, and each arm held a small green pod at its end.

"Give her one seed every day. She will survive."

"Why have they done this? Not since their first uprising have I seen them act so bold or brazen."

"It's Hillmaken. The Venom has corrupted his mind—he's desperate and is making his final move against us. He wants to rule the desert skies through your son."

"Venomous birds ruling the desert skies—this will make *everything* fall."

"That is why we must stop them."

Aridin gently woke Sparra with a kiss on her head and then gave her the first of the sacred medicine. She was disoriented but smiled when she saw their dear friend.

"We must find our prince, Honu," Sparra urged.

"We will, my queen."

Honu and Aridin stood over her until she fell asleep again. They then spent the rest of the day discussing details of their plans to stop Hillmaken.

Fifteen

The brothers sprinted up the mountain for hours. As they neared the apex of Mount Flagg, the sun had reached the midpoint of the day and was about to begin its slow descent to the west. A long run was normally not too taxing on a desert hare, but for Nick and Cade, sprinting in high altitude through thick snow while carrying a shell was exhausting.

Sam hopped out into the middle of small clearing in the trees, where he stopped and listened. "This looks just like the place the map showed."

Nick and Cade nodded in tired agreement and then squatted in the snow, slid free of the shell, and tried to catch their breath. Nick looked southward and gazed through an opening in the tree line.

"Look—you can almost see our desert from here."

Cade added, "We're so far away."

"So, now what?" Sam said nervously. He was sensing something.

"I'm not sure. Let's look around," Cade answered. "Maybe there is a cave. Let's rest, think, and eat. The coyotes should be hours away from us. We will need our strength to be ready for them."

They looked at one another, and all silently agreed that a bit of rest would do them good. They took out the last of the cactus seeds and ate them; their crunching echoed in the trees.

"I hope Olivia is all right," Sam said as he popped a handful of seeds into his mouth.

As he spoke, a rush of wind swirled through the snowy mountaintop, gently swaying the ancient pines. Loose patches of snow fell from bowed branches. The wind and the chomping of seeds hid the sound of soft footfalls. They were being watched.

Sixteen

Hundreds of years of the desert sun had baked Hillmaken's scales thick, knotty, and calloused. Over time, reddish-orange scales had grown and formed in uneven patterns and splotches across his back, head, and tail. He looked up to see one of his buzzing swarms twist through the air, a living cloud that rolled like a wave in the sky. He was close enough to Bazzering's base that he could smell the pungent odor of death, and it was a smell he liked. Hillmaken hissed and snarled as he navigated his way through muddled piles of dead snakes, lizards, toads, and a wide variety of insects. Swarms of loud flies circled the gruesome stacks of discarded recruits—those too weak for the task. Hillmaken hated weakness.

He was quite nimble, despite his stout and bulky appearance, as the Venom had also given him unnatural power and strength. He stomped his way across a dry riverbed toward a sandy bank that rose to form a small hill. He leaped several feet straight up and disappeared into a hole that was hidden below a snarl of exposed tree roots. He clawed his way through the dark tunnel until it opened up into a domed cave. The roots of cacti and shrubs growing on the hill hung like vines from its ceiling. The air was damp, and a thin mist hung around the cavern. Although there was no sunlight in the underground lair, there was a light source that threw muted shadows everywhere.

The cave floor moved like water as thousands of creatures slithered, crept, and crawled around the underground base. Most of the animals were reptile or insect, while several bloated gray rats scurried among the gathering. The horde of creatures marched in a slow, steady cadence around the green glow. All eyes were fixed on the Venom Stone as it pulsed in bubbling green water like a slow heartbeat. The rock was no bigger than a prickly pear fruit. Its smooth black surface was pocked with small craterlike holes and dimples.

"Hello, Master," Bazzering said as he hovered a safe distance over Hillmaken. "Do you like what you see? Your army is growing in strength and in number. Soon, we will be ready to march against our enemy."

Hillmaken looked up at his airborne lieutenant. "Yes, we have grown in numbers, but we are losing too many in the conversion. I thought *your* kind could adapt to the Venom better than this."

"My kind is your greatest achievement, sir. My winged warriors will serve you until their glorious death. There will be more than enough of us for our victory."

The chaotic mass of slow-marching creatures ultimately funneled into four lines that ended around the edge of the glowing water. In between the lines stood four unnaturally large brown scorpions, their sharp, sinister pincers snapping open and shut as they eyed the new recruits, their long segmented tails dangled precariously over their heads. Four animals stood at the edge of the conversion pool: a small black hornet, a dark-green snake, a thin-legged spider, and a jewel-scaled lizard.

Bazzering cried out to the recruits, "Show your dedication to the Venom. *Now!*"

The lizard was the first to step into the bubbling pool. Its eyes widened as its right claw entered the water, its scaled skin instantly lighting up with a hint of green. As it placed its other claw into the water, its pupils expanded, and yellow foam filled the corners of its mouth. The creature let out a wet hiss and then dropped dead face first into the pool. Just as the lizard fell, the closest scorpion whipped down its long tail and speared the side of the fallen lizard, its stinger easily driving through the reptile's rib cage. Green water dripped across the scorpion's heartless eyes as it tossed the dead lizard over the mass of marching creatures. A swarm of red ants mobilized and picked up the fallen recruit and carried it outside to add it to the piles of the other failed candidates. The three remaining animals were unaffected by the death of the lizard, and they all stepped into the bubbling water.

The snake hissed and violently coiled up into a writhing ball in the water. It started to grow larger, and its green scales began to transform in color. It hissed again and sprang out of the pool, landing amid the marching lines. It was no longer green but had turned white with dull-yellow diamond-shaped blotches trailing down its back. Its eyes had a hint of glowing green. It quickly slithered through the commotion and out through a tunnel to await further orders.

The spider tremored and shook when all eight legs were fully into the pool. Its skinny gray body grew bulbous and expanded with wet snaps. Its legs stretched longer and grew thicker and sharper, while two triangular red markings appeared atop its back. It looked up at Bazzering and snarled; then it leaped out of the pool and exited through the same tunnel the newly converted snake had.

The hornet was immediately altered by the pool. In seconds, it had grown to almost double its original size. Its sleek black body had become banded with yellow stripes, and its stinger had grown longer and barbed. The new flying killer looked like Bazzering and his minions.

Bazzering looked down at Hillmaken and sneered. "Three out of four, sir. Not too bad."

Hillmaken smirked. "Well done. Continue to press on. We have only days until the full moon and the fulfillment of all of our destiny."

"Yes, Hillmaken, sir. Can you stay for one more experiment?"

"Of course." A thick blob of poison dripped from Hillmaken's mouth as he smiled.

The cave grew silent except for the hum of Bazzering's wings as he hovered over the conversion pool. Every creature in the cavern continued to stare at the glow of the stone; they were all hypnotized by it.

"Bring it in!" Bazzering ordered.

The circling mass of animals stopped their march and split apart forming a clear path to the pool. Out of the darkness, a pack of arachnids appeared, sprinting toward the pool, dragging something in webs behind them. A young boar snorted and squealed as it struggled to break free from its restraints. Only its snout could be seen. The rushing line of spiders took a quick about-face away from the pool. Their webs stretched and snapped back, slinging their captive into the air. The pig hit the cavern floor with a bounce and then landed with a splash directly into the conversion pool. It let out a painful squeal that echoed throughout the cavern as the webs that held it melted away. It violently splashed in the water, bouncing off the stone several times with high-pitched yelps. Glowing green water sprayed onto the host of onlookers, and a rat collapsed dead as it was hit with a large drop of water. Finally, it stopped its convulsing, found its footing, and staggered out of the pool. All eyes shifted from the glow of the stone to the new creature that emerged from the edge of the pool. The pig's short tusks had doubled in size and now looked like snake fangs. Green venom dripped from them.

"Yes! Yes! Yes!" Hillmaken roared as he reveled in the new creation. His outburst startled every creature in the cave. "We will call it a havelin, and we need more! Yes, more war pigs!"

The Venom Stone reacted to Hillmaken's delight and pulsed with a surge of energy that instantly killed the four recruits that had just stepped into the pool. The fallen wasps and lizards were quickly speared by the scorpion undertakers and tossed back for the ants to take care of.

Bazzering circled his leader. "I am glad you approve, Master. Your army is beautiful. And it will be victorious."

Hillmaken was pleased.

Seventeen

"There must be something up here. The Pathway Stone pointed us right up to the top of Mount Flagg," Cade said.

"Whatever we're looking for, we better find it soon," Nick said as he got up from his brief respite in the snow.

A faint chorus of howls could already be heard; Ilioino and his pack had not given up their chase. A branch snapped behind the hares. They jumped up with reeds in hand and backed toward one another in a protective triangle. Perhaps the fight would be upon them sooner than they had thought.

"How did they make it up here so fast?" Sam wondered, loading a spine into his reed.

They pushed even closer together when they heard the crack of another branch. Their hearts were racing.

Deep within the trees, a voice spoke out. "Fear not, brothers."

"Who's there?" Nick said. His ears swiveled, trying to pick up the location of the voice.

Another voice answered, "We are friends and here to help you."

As if from thin air, two enormous brown bears appeared from behind a cluster of tall pines.

"I am Kodan, Elder of the Calaas bears, and this is Forina, my wife. Aridin has sent word to us that you are the chosen ones. We have come to help you on your task."

Nick responded with awe and respect. "The Pathway Stone guided us here."

Forina smiled. "So, you can use the Pathway Stone?"

Cade added, "Yes, but we don't know what we're looking for now that we're here. Maybe another clue to lead us to the Oonakestree?"

Forina assured them, "The stone has guided you correctly, young ones. The Venomous Ones have been in these peaks. Follow us, and we will take you to where the trail of their odor begins."

Sam walked closed to Forina as the two bears led them across the mountaintop to the final summit of Mount Flagg.

"We smelled their poison in the trees, but this was before we heard of the prince's abduction. We simply dismissed their presence on the mountain as an oddity—perhaps a sick creature had come into the mountain to die." Kodan paused and then sighed. "We should not have assumed their presence to be innocent. We have both fought against the Venomous Ones and should know they cannot be trusted."

"Their foulness is coming from here," Forina said and pointed to a large stone that rested on the side of the mountain.

As she said this, shrill howls arose and echoed through the trees. Ilioino and his pack were close.

"Those coyotes—they're almost here!" Cade cried.

"Do not worry about those scavengers," Kodan replied with a sly smile. He took his great paw and easily rolled away the stone, revealing a rounded opening in the side of the mountain. "The smell is coming from in there."

As the hares and bears stood looking into the hole, Ilioino and his pack burst through the trees on snowy incline and sprinted toward them.

"There is only one option, boys," Forina said.

They knew their only choice was to go into the dark, forbidding hole in the mountain.

Kodan stood up on his hind legs and roared at the advancing line of coyotes. Half of them tripped over themselves in shock and fear; several tumbled over the edge of the mountain.

"Go now!" Kodan ordered without looking back at them. "We will deal with these abominations."

Forina gazed lovingly at the hares and said, "May the Old Poem show you favor, and may light guide you in your quest."

Nick and Cade stepped down into the darkness of the hole and disappeared.

"Please, be careful," Sam said, looking up at the bears.

She bent down and kissed the top of Sam's head. "Don't you worry about us, Sam. You boys go save the desert."

Sam felt strengthened by her kindness. He smiled and then took a step down into the blackness. The yelping of yotes and the roaring of bears echoed around them as they carefully navigated their way downward. Sam had turned to look at Forina one more time when suddenly the daylight disappeared, and a pair of poison-laced jaws snapped in front of his face. Sam tripped and fell backward as the beast clawed his way into the tunnel after him. He could smell the beast's rank, hot breath as it growled and chomped at him. A small blob of the yote's drool sprayed out and landed on Sam's forehead, melting through his soft white fur and burning his skin.

"Owww!" Sam yelled in pain.

Nick and Cade turned back, only to see the snarling yote be yanked up out of the tunnel.

Kodan poked his head into the tunnel and yelled down at them. "Keep going, boys. Find the prince. Hurry! There are many of them."

Roars and yelps continued until Kodan pushed the stone back over the entrance of the tunnel. Then all light and sound disappeared.

Eighteen

Olivia and her new quail family made their way through the rocky and rolling desert. Her feet were sore, as they were not made for walking. The quail covey twisted their way through sprawling brush as they marched toward the Roos River. The thought of walking this part of the desert had never crossed her mind. She missed flying.

Normally, this part of the Desert Realm would be filled with birds of all shapes and sizes, flying and flitting about. However, this was not a normal day. Instead, the skies were filled with only dangerously deranged insects. The happy chatter of birds was replaced by the low buzz from the swirling swarms that circled in the skies over them. Olivia sighed as she looked up at an enormous swarm of venom flyers. The noise made her feel uneasy and sick. She wondered how things had gone so wrong so fast.

"Olivia." Whitt's kind voice broke her out of her skyward stare. "We are here."

They had been walking for several hours and had made their way to a valley. As they walked deeper into the canyon, the buzz of the insects began to fade, and she could hear the sounds of running water and familiar voices.

Olivia saw avian tracks everywhere, and as they rounded another corner, she could not believe her eyes. Hundreds of birds were perched on branches and stood on the shores of the small canyon. Feathered flyers of all sizes were there; from finches to falcons, the feathered ones had gathered in force. The birds were not alone; furred and scaled creatures also stood among them, while the audience of insects covered the rocky walls of the canyon. The murmur of chirps and tweets stopped, and the sea of animals parted as Aridin stepped into the gathering. He jumped up onto a large stone and addressed them.

"Our enemy plans on converting or killing every one of you and your families. There is no option but to rise up against their threat. Together we can defeat them!"

The legion of birds chirped and squawked their approval. The vast array of other animals added their own orchestra of growls, howls, and hisses. Aridin stood with them on the beaches for several more hours as they mapped out their plans to save the Desert Realm.

"Go now, and prepare for war!"

The gathering of animals broke up and left the shores in fast-moving columns. Olivia stood on the beach searching for Whitt when a voice spoke from behind her.

"Olivia."

She spun around, looked up, and then bowed. "Yes, King Aridin."

"I am thankful that you are here. The Desert Realm needs your help. The three you love need your help."

Olivia's heart swelled. "I will do whatever you ask, my king."

Nineteen

Sam continued to lead Nick and Cade down the dark incline. The faint fighting sounds of yotes and bears suddenly stopped. As a result, they also halted.

"What do we do?" Sam whispered.

Cade quietly answered, "We keep going."

Their eyes were trying to adjust to the absolute darkness of the tunnel, when with a low hum, their reeds began to emit a faint white glow. It was not much light but enough to help them avoid the rough walls and jutting rocks that surrounded them on their descent. Their new white fur also began to glow like their reeds; they looked like ghosts. They remained silent as they continued onward. Their ears independently swiveled, listening for any sound of danger. Eventually, the rocky descent leveled out into a soggy opening. The tight air of the tunnel was replaced by a cool, soft breeze. A low tumbling sound echoed around them as they stepped into a giant cavern. The glow of their reeds lit up enormous stalagmites that had grown out of the floor for thousands of years. Several were so tall that they had grown into the rocky dome of the cave.

The massive stalactites that hung from the ceiling looked like giant fangs to Sam.

"What is that smell?" Cade asked as his nose wrinkled.

He and Nick unhooked themselves and gently laid Zona's shell on the soft, muddy ground. The smell in the room was putrid, but a hint of cool, fresh air brushed against their whiskers. They all turned toward the clean smell; it was a blessing to their sensitive noses.

"There's another tunnel that leads out of here," Nick said.

Cade sniffed the air and said, "More than one."

"What is that?" Sam asked as he pointed his glowing reed toward a far corner of the cave.

"Oh my—" Nick started to say.

"Is that what I think it is?" Cade asked, his eyes widening.

"Yes!" Sam yelled.

They ran over to a large messy pile of pine needles and leaves, and lying in the middle of the makeshift nest was the Oonakestree. The egg was dirty, but its shape and structure were sound.

"We found it!" Cade said as he lowered his reed over the nest. He could not believe it was right in front of them. He reached out his paw and laid it on the egg. It was warm; that was good.

"Let's go get Zona's shell. We need to get the Oonakestree inside of it and get out of here," Nick said to Cade.

As they made their way back to the shell, they heard a faint squeaking noise from above them. They all slowly looked up and saw something green glowing.

"What is that?" Sam whispered to his brothers.

As he said this, more squeaks came from above. Now dozens of green dots appeared in the ceiling.

"Bats," Cade said, "and not the friendly kind."

As he said this, a buzzing noise had entered the cave.

"I think we have a swarm of bugs coming for us now, too," Sam said as his ears turned in the direction of the noise.

More squeaking. They looked back up to see hundreds more green eyes circling above them, so many that the entire cavern lit up with a faint green glow.

"We have to get the Oonakestree out of here!" Nick yelled.

As he said this, a hissing bat dived down at him. Nick swung at his attacker. He connected with it, knocking the bat out of the air and across the cave.

"Yes!" Cade said.

Sam pulled out a single spike from one of the crossing straps of his pack, loaded it into his reed, and aimed at the ceiling. With a deep inhale and a sharp exhale, he fired a cactus spine up into the sea of circling eyes. Several high squeaks echoed in the cave, and a hairless bat fell dead to the ground. The bat was grotesque in appearance: its once-smooth gray skin had turned rough and haggard by the Venom; its flesh looked decayed. Green blood slowly oozed from the hole the spike had left.

The cry of the wounded bats had awakened the rest of the colony, and they began to peel off the ceiling to join their poisonous clan. For a moment, it was eerily peaceful as the bats swarmed and swirled above them like a slow green tornado.

Nick and Cade followed Sam's lead and loaded their reeds. Then all three of them began to fire the spines into the circling bats. Spikes flew, and bats fell to the ground all around them. Although many were dying, there were still too many green eyes and not enough ammunition.

They killed many of the bats but were soon out of spikes. They got ready to swing at the attacking bats. Wet cracks sounded through the cave as their reeds smashed their attackers out of the air. Amid the chaos, their ears again turned toward the direction of the clean air, where the buzzing noise was getting louder and was now entering into the dome.

"Keep swinging!" Nick shouted as he obliterated several more bats with an overhead swing of his reed.

Cade swung, narrowly missing a set of wings that zipped in front of his face. He held up his glowing reed only to discover the buzzing was not a bat; it was Avery.

"Cade, we are here to help you."

Avery and several dozen hummingbirds flew straight up into the green swirl of bats. Shrill chirps and dying screeches echoed in the cave as an aerial battle of Venomous bats and brave hummingbirds ensued. Wet thuds of bats fell around them as they continued to swing at any glowing eyes that came within reach of their reeds. The frantic air battle lasted for several gruesome minutes. Then the cave fell dark and still. There were no more green eyes.

The silence was broken by buzzing and clicks from their friend Avery. "Get the prince. We will lead you out."

Nick and Cade brought the shell over to the nest, careful not to step on the dead bats that littered the floor. They laid it down next to the nest, and the shell popped open as if it was hinged on one side. Sam pulled leaves and pine needles from the nest lining the shell, preparing it for its new passenger. Nick and Cade stood across from each other on either side of the nest. They reached in and carefully lifted up the speckled egg. They carried it over and gently laid it down inside Zona's shell. Avery and his band of fighters helped Sam finish covering the Oonakestree with more protective pine needles and leaves. Once covered, they stood back and admired the beauty of the Oonakestree. Without a sound, the shell slowly closed up and sealed itself around its precious cargo.

"Amazing," Avery said.

Nick and Cade again got attached to the shell and followed Sam as he led them across the cavern floor. Sam followed the chirps of the hummingbirds. Avery led them to a corner of the cave that hid another remarkably large tunnel. As they followed him, swirls of fresh air were joined by hints of shadows and sunlight. The twisting tunnel ended abruptly into a wide but very short rocky shelf. They walked out to the ledge, inhaling the cold, clean air as deeply as they could. Billowing clouds floated all around the mountaintop, trying to hide the sun.

Avery and his band of hummingbirds landed and perched across the top of Nick's and Cade's reeds, three on each side of the front reed and two on each side of the rear, while Avery sat on top of the shell. Now out of the darkness of the cave, they could see that the hummingbirds were also sporting small packs on their backs. However, unlike the hares' packs, which carried food, reeds, and a tortoise shell, the birds' packs secured something that was much more deadly. Two delicate straps crisscrossed around their bodies, which secured two long cactus spines. The spines ran along and extended beyond the tips of their wings, they were razor sharp and stained with green blood.

"How can we get down from here?" Nick said as he peered over the edge, taking note of the boulders he could see and wary of the ones he could not.

Avery lifted off the shell, hovered, and answered, "There is a walking path down the left side of the ledge. You will have to find it."

They all looked down and saw nothing but unforgiving rocks and a steep drop.

"It should be there; it's just buried. Once you find it, you can get the Oonakestree down safely."

"*Should* be?" Sam said as he stepped away from the edge.

"I can't see anything," Nick said, looking down the ledge for the path.

A spinning gust of air whistled around the mountaintop as the clouds closed out the last hint of the sun.

Cade peered over the edge and added, "Yeah, unless we can fly, we are not going down this way."

Twenty

Olivia kept her focus on Aridin's large golden eyes as he spoke to her. She tried not to look at the king's right side, where his wing used to be.

"As you know, after your encounter with Bazzering." As he said this, a massive buzzing swarm twisted over them. "Whitt is waiting for you. Go now."

Olivia bowed to him and then turned back toward the riverbank, where Whitt and his family were waiting.

Aridin smiled as he watched the brave little bird walk away. "May the light illuminate your way."

Olivia nodded to him and then scuttled over to her covey.

Whitt called to her. "Ready for a stroll along the river, Ms. Olivia? Ready to help win a war?"

"I am!" She beamed.

The seven of them marched upriver for several hours, skirting along the shoreline, where the cool sand was a blessing on Olivia's tired feet. The sun was being challenged by billowy clouds that crept across the sky; they could all smell the rain that would soon be dropping out of the sky. Whitt stopped his quail caravan on a muddy incline near the edge of the river and looked up.

"The rain will help force the flying insects to be temporarily grounded. Rain is their enemy."

A roll of thunder boomed over them, and the rain began to fall.

"We will rest here and get nourishment."

Olivia looked down at her feet. The ground was alive with worms that wriggled and writhed, fighting against the rain that was trying to pull them down into the river. Whitt's chicks bobbed down into the bank; each of them popped back up with a beak full of squirming worms.

Although fruit was Olivia's first choice of food, she reluctantly joined Whitt and his children in pulling out the slimy snacks. She was famished from the walk.

"Eat up; get strength, as we still have many steps ahead of us." Whitt dipped down and plucked a long, fat worm from the ground, and with a quick tilt of his head, he swallowed it in one gulp.

Olivia plunged her long talons deep into the wet sand and turned over a claw full of earth that was alive with worms. She tossed them over to her adopted siblings, who quickly dug right in to the wiggling pile. She was looking out on the fast-moving river when she heard a gurgling sound at her feet, and thick muddy bubbles began popping up around her.

"Big worms? Olivia asked.

The bubbles grew.

"Children, come to me," Whitt said as he hurried up the bank. His chicks obediently sprinted up the bank and huddled up behind him. "Olivia!"

"What is it?" Olivia asked as she backed her way up from the river.

Three large bubbles pushed up out of the shore, forcing out more patches of worms.

When Olivia reached Whitt, she asked again, "What is it?"

More bubbles popped, revealing six yellow amphibian eyes.

The birds continued to back their way up the bank when three well-fed toads clawed their way out of the wet embankment. The largest of them made its way free of the earth and croaked out a loud *"Bwaaaaap!"*

The other two toads each echoed the call as they freed themselves from the muddy bank. *"Bwaaaaap! Bwaaaaap!"*

"All of you, run!"

Olivia followed Whitt and his chicks out of the bank and away from the river. The toads began to chase after them. Despite their round and awkward appearance, they were surprisingly quick. One of them still had several worms clumped in mud across its bony head as it hopped after the birds.

Whitt and his quail family skillfully sprinted into the desert, avoiding rocks and cutting through the cactus and low, dense brush. Quail were made for this type of escape, and Whitt had a keen eye for the right path. But Olivia struggled to keep up and for a moment lost sight of them. She fought the urge to open her wings and take flight.

The three rotund toads had given up on the quail, and now their collective focus was solely on Olivia. They croaked as they chased her. *"Bwaaaaap!"*

Whitt stopped, and fear gripped him when he turned back and could not see her. "Olivia!"

The rain suddenly stopped as fast as it had started, and the sun broke out from a long, thin opening in the clouds. The desert sparkled as sunlight reflected through the prisms of raindrops that hung everywhere from spikes and leaves. Olivia continued to run toward Whitt's voice while trying to navigate the tight paths. The toads were gaining on her.

She made a quick cut right, causing one of the toads to trip over himself and crash into a thick spiked cholla. The toad roared in pain as it tried to peel itself free from the plant.

"Bwaaaaap! Bweeeeep! Bwaaaaaaap!"

It finally succeeded in tearing itself off the cacti but fell in pain and gave up. The toad's bumpy back was covered with dozens of long yellowish spines. Dark-green blood oozed from its skin.

"Olivia, here!"

The sky brightened again as the sun fought away the rain clouds. Olivia could still not see the quail. She struggled to make her way through the desert as the two remaining toads closed in on her. Whitt and his clan sat atop a small hill and looked down in fear and horror as both toads leaped at the running owl.

"Bwaaaaap!"

Her survival instincts took over, and she opened her wings and lifted straight into the air, narrowly escaping their snapping jaws. The toads croaked in dismay and looked up as the little gray owl flew away from them.

"Bwaaaaap! Bwaaaaap!"

"Olivia," Whitt shouted from the hilltop. "Get to the ground!"

She caught sight of the covey and flew toward them just as a twisting shadow appeared from behind the rain clouds. It was a swarm, and it screamed toward her. Before her talons could hit the ground, the army of wasps and hornets encircled her, snatched her up, and flew away with her.

Whitt and his family stood in stunned silence. Olivia the quail-owl was gone.

Twenty-One

Large snowflakes floated down around them as the icy wind danced across their white coats. Hares and hummingbirds looked out over the lofty ledge, which was gradually being frosted with a thin layer of snow.

Avery chirped to his feathered companions, who replied with a single acknowledging click and then flew away into the clouds. Cade turned toward Avery and lifted his right paw as if to ask a question.

Avery spoke again, this time in common tongue. "We will spread the word to the Elders that you have the Oonakestree. You are to take him back to Honu's lair, where he will remain protected until he is born. You must leave *now*. The stone still blocks your exit out of the tunnel. So unless you can move it, you need to find the path down. Just get the Oonakestree off this mountain." He did not wait for their response before flying away.

Nick, Cade, and Sam stood in the swirling snow and watched him disappear into the clouds. Nick spoke first. "Let's go see if we can pry out that stone. I still don't see how we can navigate that drop, especially without knowing where the path is."

Sam responded, "I'll go down and look for it. We'll find it."

Cade looked at his brothers. "Avery said something before they flew away. He told them each to go seek out the Elders and have them send any help they could to us. But I thought he said something about a snake."

"Snake?" Sam asked, turning to Cade. "Snake? How could any snake be anywhere near snow? It would freeze. And why wouldn't Avery tell us?"

"Hmm, I *thought* that's what he said." Cade shifted his gaze out into the clouds as he replied, "Maybe I misunderstood, or maybe he doesn't want to scare us."

"Snake or no snake, we need to get the Oonakestree off this mountain. Let's try to move that stone first. And if we can't, we come back and look for the trail that Avery said is down there somewhere."

They turned away from the steep ledge and began to walk back into the dark tunnel that led to the bat cave. Sam's reed immediately began to glow as they stepped into the twisting passageway and headed back toward the open dome; this time, it glowed even brighter. As they made their way through the final turns, the horrible smell of the bats hit their noses again. This time the stench was mixed with venom and death.

"Oh man, it's so awful," Sam said as his stomach did a small flip in protest of the odor. He brought his arm up across his face in hopes of blocking out the smell.

All three of their reeds were now glowing brightly, illuminating the carnage of the aerial battle. The clumsy bats had not stood a chance against the sharp spinning spines on the hummingbirds' wings. Pieces and parts of bat were everywhere in the dome.

With mindful steps, Sam cleared their path across the floor, pushing bat remnants out of their way with his reed. They stepped up into the passageway and made their way back toward the exit. Sam stopped in front of the large stone. He turned back to ask how they were going to move it, when the light that radiated from their reeds began to dance on across Zona's shell, as if it was alive. Sam squinted and stepped in between his brothers to examine the shell.

"Wait! Zona's shell—there's some kind of writing on it, and it's moving!" Sam exclaimed. He lifted his reed over the shell and saw symbols moving across its surface like a rolling wave. Some he was familiar with; some he wasn't.

Cade asked, "What does it say?"

Sam started to circle his reed over Zona's shell, trying to discern the glowing cryptograms that stirred across it.

"Hold on, it looks like a poem.

Slave to the stone, the henchman of hate
ruling the desert, he sees as his fate
twisting of nature, the conversion of life,
shifting of balance, the bringing of strife.
His demise will be fed through rivers and flows
and crushed out like night, by the old stone that grows."

As Sam uttered the last words, the glowing symbols disappeared. "Dang, it's gone."

Cade repeated, "Henchman of hate? Hillmaken?"

Nick replied, "We can't worry about him now. We have to get out the Oonakestree out of here."

Nick and Cade unhooked themselves and carefully laid Zona's shell on the rocky floor. The tunnel lit up as a blue light flashed across the crown of the shell, and then a radiant shape jumped onto the tunnel wall and flew back toward the domed cave. It was an owl.

"Olivia! Did you guys see that?"

"See what?" Cade said as he held his reed up to the boulder blocking their exit.

"An owl! Never mind. Hey, I can smell clean air again." Sam walked over and pressed his nose up to the crack between the stone and the tunnel wall. He inhaled deeply.

Nick and Cade followed his lead, and soon, all three had their noses pressed up against the tiny openings around the exit-blocking stone. Their lungs rejoiced in the cool, clean air. From outside the tunnel, three small puffs of breath could be seen steaming in and out.

"I think that maybe Avery was right. I think I smell snake too," Cade said in between breaths.

Sam again turned back to them. "Snake?"

"A snake in snow, at this altitude? No. Even Eelion couldn't make it in these conditions. Maybe Cade misunderstood. There is no snake, Sam. Now let's see if we can move this rock."

Nick took one last breath of fresh air and then jammed his reed near the base of the rock. The rock shifted.

"Nice work, Nick. I think we *can* pry it out," Cade said as he too forced his reed into a small opening. The boulder shifted again.

Nick and Cade pushed down on their reeds. The large rock slowly began tilting outward. Another wave of cool, clean air rushed in around them.

"I think I do smell snake," Sam reasserted as his nose wrinkled up and examined the air.

His nose was right. There was a snake on the snowy mountaintop, and it was Eelion. The giant rattler was coiled up just outside of the tunnel on the other side of the boulder. His forked tongue darted in and out as he tasted their breath through the cold air. Eelion's eyes gleamed with anticipation. He had to sit on his rattled tail to conceal the sound of his excitement.

Sam said, "I bet Eelion is right outside this rock waiting to eat us and take the Oonakestree."

"Sam, we can move the rock, but we need your help," Nick said as he ignored the comment and continued to pry the rock forward.

"Fine!"

In his frustration and with all his might, Sam swung his reed, striking the middle of the rock. The impact of the reed on the stone was a thunderous *crack*! The deafening sound was accompanied by a blinding flash as the boulder and the three reeds lit up as if electrified with blue lightning. Then the brilliant light

shattered into a buzzing eruption as the boulder exploded outward into thousands of electrically charged pieces of rock. White-hot jagged stones ripped through the majestic trees that grew across the mountaintop, sending dozens of them tumbling to the ground.

Eelion was much too close to escape the rocky explosion. The force blew him violently back toward the shredded tree line. The electric stones tore through what he had come to believe were impenetrable scales. He hissed in pain as he flew through the air and then shrieked as he crashed violently into the smoldering stump of a large tree.

Nick, Cade, and Sam stood up, shaking away the ringing from their ears, and then stepped out of the tunnel. The explosion had left the mountaintop in a thick smoky mist, and they could not see more than a few inches in front of themselves.

"Guys, get the shell loaded again. Let's get going; we have a way down!" Sam said, waving his reed in the snowy air around them.

Nick and Cade had become rather efficient at securing themselves to and detaching from Zona's shell. Mere seconds after Sam had made his request, the shell was resting on reeds and on their backs.

Nick looked out on the cloudy mountaintop and nodded to Cade. "We can go back down the way we came. The path was straight away from the tunnel across the narrow pass. Let's go. We will find a way to cross the river once we get down."

Cade said jokingly, "We could always swim again."

They stepped into the snowy haze and made their way toward the path but froze when they heard the snap of a breaking branch. They stood still and said nothing. Their white coats hid them in the smoke and swirling snow.

"Something's out there," Nick whispered as his ears scanned the surroundings. "Do you guys see anything?"

A rush of air ran across the mountaintop and cleared away most of the hanging haze. They were amazed at the destruction they saw. Giant trees had been blown apart, leaving smoldering stumps and mounds of burning branches. If snow had not been falling, the entire mountaintop would likely have ignited from the explosion.

Cade replied, "I think we're OK. I don't see anything—just a bunch of broken trees. Plus, I don't think anything could have survived that." His nose twitched as he tried to smell through the thick air.

Another branch cracked, and Sam brought his reed back over his right shoulder, ready to swing. The silence was broken by a series of fast, loud pops that rattled through the air, and Eelion slithered out from out of the smoky tree line and coiled up in front of them. His forked tongue darted in and out, each time leaving a wisp of circling steam.

Sam took several slow steps back until his pack bumped up against Zona's shell and he was standing in between Nick and Cade, who were now squatted down and ready to sprint.

"Well, it looks like it was hares after all," Eelion hissed at them. "Impressive, I must say."

Cade spoke with disgust. "Eelion."

"Have we met before?" he asked as his jaw unhinged into an evil smile.

He did know them.

Eelion had always been a terrifying sight, but now he was both terrifying and gruesome. The explosion had left him with only his left eye; the right had been shredded off by one of the electric rocks. Only a hollow and bloody socket remained. Deep wounds oozed and bled across the parts of his body that had been facing the tunnel. Several of the wounds were so deep that the muscle had been burned or torn completely away, exposing the thin bones that formed his long, twisting body. Any other snake would have died from the force of the explosion. However, his rattled tail was still fully intact, and it let off another set of loud, quick pops. Branches and twigs snapped as dozens of his venomous yotes appeared from the tree line and began to slink toward them. The pack tried to hold in their whimpers of anticipation as the exhilaration of the chase and the smell of hares danced in their nostrils. The yotes could not contain their excitement, and they began to howl. Their cries grew louder and echoed across the mountaintop.

"Back into the cave!" Nick shouted.

Eelion's rattle cracked out to three loud pops, and then his pack broke through the tree line and sprinted toward the hares. Eelion lunged at Sam, who had stepped out to face the attacking snake while swinging his reed with all his might. The very tip of the reed smashed into Eelion's remaining eye with a dull crack, sending him twisting backward in pain, crashing harshly into a pile of smoldering rocks and branches. He quickly gathered himself back into a coil and tried to shake away the stars that flashed in his remaining eye.

"Get them! Get them!" Eelion hissed in anger and pain.

His yotes howled as they raced across the mountaintop toward them. Nick and Cade spun around with the shell and disappeared back into the opening of the tunnel. As they did so, they both shouted, "Sam!"

Their yell broke Sam's gaze at Eelion. Sam slowly lowered his reed, turned, and ran down into the darkness after his brothers.

Eelion regained enough of his sight to see three of his deranged yotes reach the entrance at the same time. In their zeal, they dove headfirst into the tunnel, only to crash into each other and get wedged firmly in the rocky opening. The remaining pack could not slow in time and smashed headfirst into the three stuck yotes. The crazed canines bounced off one another and the mountain wall as they mindlessly chased after the smell of their prey. The entire pack clawed, scratched, and pushed into the tunnel until their force finally broke the wedge free. One by one, they sprinted down the passageway after the hares.

"They're coming!" Sam warned. He caught up with his brothers just as they entered the domed cave.

"Jump when we get to the ledge—we should be able to clear the first ridge of stones. Then hopefully it will be all snow for us after that. It's our only chance. We can't fight them all," Nick shouted as they sprinted across the cave. Their reeds again began to glow.

"I smell the fresh air. It's this way!" Cade yelled.

Eelion's yotes poured out of the tunnel into cavernous dome, chasing blindly after them, running over and through the piles of dead bats.

"They're catching us!" Sam yelled.

"Keep going, Sam. You need to grab the shell and hang on when we get to the edge."

"Are we really jumping? Again?"

Cade and Nick replied in unison, "Yes."

They navigated their way through the last turns that led to the drop, and the pack was on them. As they sprinted out of the tunnel across the snow-covered ledge, Sam stowed his reed and jumped on top of the shell, holding on with both paws.

Ilioino and his band of yotes continued to chase after the hares' scent, howling and yelping as they unknowingly ran toward their doom. One after the other, they sprinted off the ledge of the mountain and crashed down into the jagged boulders that were hidden under the snow. None of them survived, not even Ilioino. Fortunately, the hares did not suffer the same fate.

They sailed out over the edge of the mountain, hoping their jump was enough to make it over the first rows of jagged stones that peeked up out of the snow. As they flew, the wind found its way into the nooks and folds of Nick and Cade's packs, which

expanded with a pop and came alive. Thin white tendrils of silk exploded from their packs and then spread across the reeds like water. These silken vines wove themselves together across the underside of Zona's shell until they formed an airtight wing. Another gust of wind came; this time it lifted them straight up into the air.

Sam could not believe it. "We're flying!"

Eelion slid to a stop as the last chasing yote tumbled down the steep ledge. His rattle stopped as he glared up in rage at the hares, who glided away and disappeared into the clouds.

Twenty-Two

Olivia awoke with blurred vision and a dizzy head. Slow-moving shadows crept across the ceiling above her. She attempted to get to her feet but could only roll over onto her side. A low green light was reflecting in her eyes. From her neck to her knees, she had been bound up by thick strands of spider webs that kept her wings firmly pressed to her sides. As her eyes adjusted to the darkness, she gasped when she saw thousands of creatures circling around the cavern. Hisses, buzzes, and shrill reptilian screams rang out as animals were either converted or killed by the Venom Stone's powerful glowing green water.

"Ah, our friend is finally awake." Bazzering smiled. "I thought you were going to sleep and miss all of the fun. Don't you want to see the army that is going to destroy you and your kind—all of you arrogant creatures who rejected the way of Venom?"

He let out a short high-pitched buzz, and two enormous yellow jackets appeared over him; they were easily twice his size. They flew toward Olivia, pulled up, and landed upside down on the ceiling above her. Their yellow segmented bodies reflected the dull glow of the Venom Stone; their black translucent wings had yellow spots blotted across them. Bazzering clicked again, and the two yellow jackets swooped down and grabbed on to the sides of Olivia's webbed cocoon, lifting her up onto her feet.

"You will want to watch this," he said, hovering over her.

Four sleek brown lizards with long tails stepped into the pool at the same time. The largest of them instantly fell dead with a wet cough. A scorpion quickly stabbed and discarded it. The other three lizards shrieked and convulsed in the stone's green water. Half of their tails fell off, and they began to transform into thick dark-gray creatures. Gnarled orange scales bubbled up across their backs and legs. They looked like small versions of Hillmaken.

"Excellent," Bazzering whispered to himself.

Now that Olivia was upright, she could see the Venom Stone over the marching animals. It pulsed as her eyes fell upon it and made her feel dizzy again, but she could not look away. All sound disappeared; she could not hear the yellow jackets that still hovered over her or Bazzering and his ongoing declaration of the Venomous One's grand plans. Her vision began to tunnel in on the Venom Stone, and she could not look away. Darkness and fear closed in around her. Finally, her focus was broken by a shrill squeal of a rat that stepped in the pool. She turned her head away and closed her eyes, trying to forget the sight of the dying rat. Two of the undertakers whipped down their long tails and pierced away its last breath, and then each pulled away, tearing the rodent in two. When Olivia opened her eyes, Bazzering was hovering directly in front of her.

"Isn't their conversion beautiful? Those who accept the conversion will know the truth, and it gives them power. Now, my dear, you will join them."

He floated up over her and addressed the two wasps.

"Put her in!"

"Birds will not accept the Venom like you did!" Olivia screeched at him, trying to hide her fear.

With a nod from Bazzering, the two yellow jackets hoisted her up over the gathering of creatures and carried her toward the conversion pool.

"You are wrong, little owl. We have a bird of Venom patrolling the skies right now. You can join him. Become one of our winged warriors." Bazzering could not hold back his excitement, and the Venom Stone pulsed again.

"No, you lie! No bird would accept the Venom!"

"Dear, dear, I do not lie. Why would we want to steal the Oonakestree if we are not sure a bird could survive the conversion? We know now that we must get them when they are *very* young."

Olivia was lowered down between two of the scorpions at the edge of the pool, so close that her long claws hung over the rim, almost touching the bubbling green water.

"Do not be afraid, little feathered one. The stone will give you strength." Bazzering snickered as he slowly circled above her. "Or it will kill you!"

A low humming noise flew into the cave. It was a large Venom-mutated dragonfly. The insect circled around the cave several more times and then darted straight toward Olivia before it turned up and landed on the ceiling directly above Bazzering. The uneven segments of its long body were lumpy gray and were covered with jagged red lines; its wings were a translucent green. The dragonfly swiveled its head toward Bazzering and spoke in a series of high-pitched buzzes and pops.

Bazzering turned away from Olivia and tilted his head toward the news. "The Oonakestree has been lost? How can that be?"

More clicks from the dragonfly further enraged Bazzering. "Not lost but stolen?"

Still more clicks and a long, uninterrupted series of high buzzes.

"Prophecy? Hares?"

Olivia's heart filled with joy, and she felt a spark of courage rise inside her. The Elders had been right. Nick, Cade, and Sam were the three the Old Poem spoke of, and they had somehow rescued the prince. Maybe the desert could be saved after all.

The marching lines of animals pushed forward; snakes, lizards, and creeping critters slithered and crawled toward the pool and into Olivia. She pushed back against them with all her strength, her talons burying into the soft ground. She would not be able to hold them all back. The little owl wished her wings were free so she could fly away from this horrible place.

"Hares?" Bazzering asked himself.

Olivia could not hold back the line of animals, and she began to fall into the pool.

"Wait! Stop her!" Bazzering yelled.

The hovering yellow jackets darted down and snatched Olivia up just before she fell into the bubbling water.

"Our dear little owl has friends that are hares. Hmm, I bet they would do anything to save her. We will bring her to the Great Lake with us."

He looked up at the dragonfly that still clung to ceiling above them. It buzzed a quick response.

"Yes, inform Hillmaken we will begin our march with the Venom Stone to the Great Lake, and we will bring the friend of the hares. With or without the Oonakestree, Hillmaken will destroy those who oppose him. Once we bless the Great Lake with the power of Venom, all animals of the Desert Realm will come to depend on its power. Those who don't will leave—leave or die."

Twenty-Three

Three hares and a tortoise shell sailed on a wing of reed and silk as the wind carried them in and out of billowy clouds and away from Mount Flagg. They quickly figured out that shifting their weight and adjusting their long ears controlled the pitch and angle of their shell glider. Sam was still stretched across the top, holding on tightly with both paws. They soared over the Roos River, high above the large rock that they had jumped from.

"Look! I see the reflection of the Great Lake," Sam said as he pointed to a glimmering body of water far off in the distance.

"Yes, Honu's lair is not far from there. We need to get the Oonakestree to him," Nick added.

"We can fly right to him!" Sam said with a wide grin, made even wider by the wind in his face.

Cade caught a glimpse of a dark rolling cloud in the sky, and it was flying toward them. "Guys, we have a problem. Look!"

Nick and Sam turned their attention to the fast-approaching armada.

Nick yelled, "A swarm! We need to get to the ground quickly. If it thinks we're a bird, we will be bug food."

The wave of insects continued its rolling and twisting toward them. The three of them shifted their weight forward and extended their ears straight up into vees. The resistance slowed their flight, and they began to descend in a fast, tight spiral. The Venom flyers did not slow their chase, and as they got closer, the deep buzz of the swarm grew louder—too loud.

"Hurry! We have to get down," Sam said, leaning over the front of the shell to make sure his brothers could hear him.

"Keep leaning forward. If we can beat the swarm to the ground, maybe we'll be safe," Cade said.

"I'm leaning!" Sam yelled, his ears still in a vee. "And how do we know we'll be safe? How do we know they won't attack us, flying or not?"

They continued to circle downward. Nick and Cade scanned the desert for a safe place to land their makeshift glider.

"They are only looking for birds, not flying hares," Nick tried to reassure Sam. However, he wasn't sure that would be true this time.

"But we *are* a big bird right now!"

The ground came fast as they descended. The swarm's buzz grew to a deafening level as it closed in on them.

Sam looked up into the swarm as it was about to engulf them. Nick's and Cade's paws hit the ground with a bump, but they instantly found their footing and sprinted, keeping their momentum from flipping them over. Sam had ducked his face and ears forward on the shell during the landing. Nick and Cade skidded to a stop, and the attacking swarm broke apart like a giant wave on the desert floor around them. There was no flying prey now, so the insects dispersed and zipped back up into the sky. The desert suddenly became quiet.

"Are they gone?" Sam asked with his face still down on the shell.

"I think so," Nick said, looking up. The swarm continued to vanish into the sky.

Cade tried to catch his breath. "I can't believe it. They should have had us."

"Remember what Honu said. They can't think for themselves," Nick replied.

Sam jumped down from the shell. "The birds must still be hiding. It's so quiet." He hopped over to his brothers and then added, "Hey, guys, we've changed again."

Cade and Nick looked at Sam and saw the transformation: their white fur had changed back to their original brownish-gray desert-ready coats.

Sam leaned down and peered into the front opening of Zona's shell. He could see the egg safely tucked into his bed of pine needles and leaves. He smiled as he said, "The Oonakestree is OK!"

Nick and Cade both felt a bit of relief but then noticed something in the sky coming toward them.

"Is that a—" Cade began.

"Bird?" Nick finished his brother's sentence.

Sam turned around. "A bird?"

"Maybe we did it. Maybe there won't be a war. Maybe we stopped it," Nick said with hopeful enthusiasm.

Cade echoed Nick's feeling of hope. "Yes, we rescued the prince. The swarms are gone, and we see a bird in the sky!"

With the setting sun behind it, the avian silhouette soared gracefully toward them. The bird's broad wingspan looked like that of a large eagle. It was a peaceful and beautiful sight and a relief to see a bird in the sky, not a swarm.

"Maybe it's the queen coming to see her son," Sam surmised as he walked away from his brothers in the direction of the approaching bird. He brought his arms up over his head and waved them back and forth. "Right here!" Sam then spun back around to face his brothers and said with his widest grin, "Can you believe this? Did we just save the desert?"

Upon the hares' landing, the silken vines had unwound and unrolled from the reeds, weaving themselves back into the packs, just as they had been. Nick and Cade detached themselves from the shell, still watching the oncoming bird.

"Wait," Nick said as he thought he saw something glowing.

"Wait, what? I mean, we're going to be heroes, right?" Sam looked up into the heavens and added, "Mom and Dad would be proud of us."

"Sam!" Cade and Nick shouted at the same time.

"What?" Sam said, still grinning ear to ear.

With a deafening screech, Hillmaken's vultch swooped down and grabbed Sam's reed, which was secured horizontally through the top of his pack like a perch. Sam's smile was replaced by confusion as he was snatched up in the air. Nick and Cade leaped up, hoping to grab his legs, but each touched only the tips of his toes as he shot up into the sky.

"Sam, hang on!" Nick shouted.

As Sam continued skyward, he looked up at his abductor and saw that it was not Sparra but rather a Venomous bird. Its body was similar in shape and size to that of a large raptor, but everything else was all gruesome and wrong. There were no plumage on his head and neck, only dead, lumpy skin. The feathers that ran under its wings looked like long snake scales; its eyes were reptilian. Dozens of razor-sharp fangs jutted out in all directions from its haggard gray beak; several sprouted out just above its right eye. Sam thought about trying to slip out of his pack to escape, but he was already too high. Any drop from this height would kill him.

"What was that thing? A Venomous bird?" Cade yelled.

Nick wasn't sure. "A Venomous bird?"

"We have to get Sam!" Cade implored.

The vultch let out a long screech, and another swarm of wasps formed out of the sky and fell in behind the Venom bird as it flew off with its prize. Nick and Cade kept their focus upward and tried to follow the path of their kidnapped brother. However, in an instant, the sun dipped beneath the horizon, and darkness ate up the light. Stars popped on across the new night sky, and Sam could not be seen anymore.

Nick and Cade said nothing as tears filled their eyes. The silence of the desert was broken by the loud buzz of another swarm flying over them. Neither looked up as it rolled by. They were too heartbroken to be afraid.

"What do we do now?"

Nick tried to sound strong as he wiped a falling tear away from his cheek. "We have to find Honu. We bring the Oonakestree to him, and he will help us find Sam."

Twenty-Four

B azzering hovered over his marching army and was filled with pride. Visions of his war heroics and future fame played in his mind. His horde had made excellent time that day; they had slithered, crept, and crawled across the ever-changing terrain with little rest. The unforgiving sun never yielded its inspection of them, and dozens of warriors died on the march. Dozens didn't worry him; the Venomous Ones had thousands—probably millions, including all the flyers. Bazzering sent word that they would stop for camp, as they were now just a morning's march away from their destiny at the Great Lake. It was the site Hillmaken had declared to be the grave of the deniers and the cornerstone of the new Venom Empire. The ground under them had become more rock than dirt, and the air cooled quickly without the sun. The dropping temperatures naturally slowed down the cold-blooded soldiers.

The Venom Stone was brought into the center of the camp by four large gray lizards who carried it in on a gnarled nest of ocotillo branches spread across their backs in uneven rows.

Although it was not large, the stone's weight forced the barbs of the branches to puncture the scales of the lizards. Blood oozed down their backs in dark-green stripes. They stopped and knelt, setting the makeshift transport down. The stone lit up and melted its way through the carrier, softly rolling to the ground with a hiss.

Bazzering gathered his flying lieutenants and clicked several orders to them. "Rest well tonight, and dream of your glory—the glory Venom will bring to us all!"

His winged subordinates disappeared into the night to inform the troops it was time to settle in. Tomorrow, they would march up the eastern shore of the Great Lake and flank their enemy, forcing them into the jaws of Hillmaken's ground forces.

Bazzering's troops had marched together all day, united and intertwined among diverse species with no incident. However, as they broke off to rest for the night, they gathered among their own kind in frantic masses.

Snakes of all shapes, sizes, and colors began to huddle together in what could only be described as a writhing reptilian blob that hissed as it sluggishly rolled around the new camp. Rattles popped and fangs snapped as they cozied together.

The Venom lizards also began to group together. They clawed and gnashed in a frenzy, each trying to reach the top of the ever-moving pile. Toes and tails were bitten off in the chaos; several lizards even died. But unlike the blob of snakes that continued to roll around the camp, the lizards finally stopped, forming a large, heaving mound.

The millions of red ants that had silently marched along with Bazzering's army quickly burrowed underground as they looked for shelter and warmth.

Thousands of centipedes began to gather together; they formed into several slow-moving circular masses. The moon's glow reflected off them like dark pools of swirling water, an oasis of bugs.

The Venom spiders that crept among them took refuge in any nearby tree, bush, or cactus. Most spun quick, crude webs to rest on, while some of the larger spiders dug out and disappeared into sandy burrows.

The few rats that had survived the day's journey aimlessly roamed in a venom-fueled daze among the now-segregated camp. Most of them would die before morning. Hillmaken was right: they were weak.

Bazzering circled over the Venom Stone, staring at it the pulsing green rock.

"Bring the bird to me."

The four large yellow jackets that had carried Olivia throughout the day began to lower her to the ground. She was still wrapped in her webbed cocoon.

"You will sleep here, next to the stone. It will protect you." Bazzering laughed.

The yellow jackets bit through the supporting strands of web that held Olivia in the air, and she fell to the ground with a soft thud. She was now just feet away from the Venom Stone, whose pulsing energy immediately made her feel weak and frightened.

Bazzering clicked out several long high-pitched pops, and all of the red-legged centipedes broke from their small circles and began crawling toward the Venom Stone and Olivia. She closed her eyes as the wave of crawlers closed in on her. She was sure they would swallow her up and kill her with painful bites and stings. Instead, they marched under her and lifted her up off the ground as they formed one large revolving centipede moat around the stone. She floated across the top of them like a log bobbing along on a river. She looked up at the night sky and focused on one brilliant shining star; then she closed her eyes and prayed she would survive the night.

"Yes, you sleep well, little birdy. Tomorrow is a big day for the desert," Bazzering boldly told his captive before flying off into the night. He would fly to Hillmaken to share news of the captive and for a final review of their war strategy. The plan was quite simple: convert all to the Venom, and kill those who didn't comply.

The night's cool air had slowed down the entire camp, except for the circling mass of centipedes that continued to orbit Olivia slowly around the Venom Stone. Two of Bazzering's henchmen flew in from the darkness and hovered over her; they had been ordered to keep watch over her while Bazzering was away.

"Why does he make us watch this bird?" the larger of the two asked his fellow guard.

"Exactly. Why? Look at it. It's bound up and going nowhere," the other replied.

"Except in circles."

They laughed as they hovered over her.

The smaller of the two guards lowered itself in front of Olivia and asked, "You're not going anywhere, are you?"

She kept her eyes closed and ignored him as she continued to slowly bob around on the circling centipede eddy. A small bubbling pool had formed around the Venom Stone.

"Yes, sleep well, feathered one."

Olivia's eyes popped open as she and the guards turned toward a shrill screech that ripped through the night air.

"A bird?" she whispered to herself and felt a spark of hope rise.

The larger guard said, "It's the vultch."

"I don't trust that thing; it's still a bird," the smaller guard said as he leaned into his partner. "Birds are not worthy of the Venom, if you ask me."

"Look—it has something."

The vultch soared down toward the base with Sam still hanging helplessly from his pack. It slowed its steep descent by extending and flapping its massive wings, which caused a small cloud of dust to spread through the camp. But instead of landing, it let go of the reed, dropping Sam down into the middle of the camp, between the stone and a large mound of sleeping lizards.

"A hare?" one of the lieutenants asked his partner.

"I heard Bazzering and Hillmaken discussing a prophecy about the Oonakestree. I think they said something about hares. Or was it bears?"

"Either way, we need to tell Bazzering. You stay here and watch over the little bunny. I will go inform him."

The wasp did not wait for a reply before flying off into the night. He hoped he would be rewarded for bringing Bazzering the news of another prisoner.

▲ ▲ ▲

Sam scanned the camp, trying to get a bearing on where he was and hoping there might be an ally nearby. Olivia came into view, and his eyes lit up with joy and then dread as he saw his beloved friend afloat on a surf of centipedes.

"Olivia?" he whispered.

She opened her eyes but thought she was dreaming.

"Olivia?"

"Sam!" She was overjoyed to see him and relieved he was real.

"I'll get you out of there."

"Watch it, rabbit!" the remaining wasp guard shouted as it darted down and hovered in front of Sam before he could step toward Olivia.

"I'm a hare!" he declared.

He was not scared; this single hovering insect was nothing compared to what he and his brothers had faced over the past several days. A gust of dry wind rushed through the camp, strong enough to push the yellow jacket backward. Its right wing sparked as it made contact with the Venom Stone, forcing the insect to the ground. Its wing was badly damaged and looked burned.

"Fine, Mr. Hare! You can join your owl friend. The spiders will wrap you up until Bazzering gets back."

He snickered then turned away from Sam toward a patch of tall saguaros, where many of the spiders had taken residence for the night. It tilted its head and let out two long, low clicks in an effort to wake the web weavers. There was no movement on the cactus, so it clicked again. Before it could finish, Sam's reed smashed into the wasp's head, splintering its right antenna and dropping the creature motionless to the ground. Sam stood over it with his reed resting on his right shoulder, ready to swing at the slightest twitch from the wasp.

"Sam," Olivia uttered as quietly as she could. She was now rolled onto her side.

Fortunately, neither the centipedes nor any of the resting mounds of soldiers seemed to notice or care that their commander was now lying in a heap next to their all-powerful stone.

"Olivia, hang on," he whispered.

As she floated toward him, Sam extended his reed out over the swirling bugs and slid it through a small loop in her cocoon. He carefully lifted her up off the creeping bugs and laid her down as easily as he could. He was out of spines and needed something sharp to cut her free from the webs. He hopped over to the saguaros and popped off a long, sharp spine with his reed. The noise awakened the spiders.

Sam quickly returned and cut through the webbing. As soon as her wings were free, she wrapped them around him in a loving embrace.

"I am so glad to see you."

"Are you OK?"

"Yes, I'm fine. Where are Nick and Cade? What about the Oonakestree?" Olivia's voice rose in excitement.

"Sh. I don't know where they are, but they have the Oonakestree. We were heading to Honu's when that thing snatched me."

"You have the Oonakestree?"

"Sh! Yes, I will tell you all about it later; we have to get out of here."

A chorus of hisses rose from behind them as pack of large spindly legged spiders crept out of the darkness.

"Olivia?"

The noise awakened the lizards, who rolled out of their sleeping mounds and began to scramble aimlessly in all directions across the camp. They clawed and bit anything in their way as they blindly scuttled over their sleeping comrades. The ruckus caused the entire camp to come alive, and tempers flared. The Venom Stone pulsed its approval of the chaos. Snakes attacked scorpions, centipedes attacked lizards, and soon, the entire camp was battling itself.

As the confusion set in, Olivia grabbed Sam's pack, and they flew away from the camp.

Twenty-Five

Bazzering landed in the middle of Hillmaken's base. Like his camp members, these soldiers had also gathered together and huddled up by ilk. This base was the Venomous One's main land force, twice the size of Bazzering's.

Danix scurried out from behind a mound of sleeping snakes.

"Bazzering?" Danix hissed. He hated the wasp. "Why do you leave your base and the Venom Stone?"

"I have important news to tell our master. So creep along, and go get him," Bazzering snapped back with disdain that he did not bother to hide from the scorpion.

"What news?" Danix's pincers clicked with excitement.

"I am bound to Hillmaken, not to his errand boy." Bazzering's wings came to life, and he lifted off the ground and hovered over Danix. "Go get him!"

Danix's tail began to sway slowly above his head. He was inching toward Bazzering when another voice was heard.

"I am here, Bazzering. What is the news you bring to me?"

Bazzering spun toward the voice. His wings stopped, and he landed in front of his master and bowed. Danix opened his fanged mouth in a slimy smile; he enjoyed seeing the arrogant bug humbled.

"Get up and speak." Hillmaken's voice lacked any hint of patience.

"I have tremendous news, Hillmaken, sir—news that I know will exemplify my dedication and commitment to the Venom and to you, Lord Hillmaken."

Danix let out another giggle at Bazzering's blatant pandering but was silenced by a quick glance from Hillmaken.

"I know about the capture of one little owl. I hope this is not why you left your watch over the Venom Stone." Hillmaken's thick curved claws dug into the ground as his anger swelled.

"Sir, my men have my base secured, and the Venom Stone is safe."

Danix cackled out loud, and his feet kicked up sand in excitement as he felt Hillmaken's anger build.

Bazzering nervously changed his tone. "I mean *your* base is under control, sir. And the Venom Stone is secure. *Your* troops are resting, and the spiders are out on patrol. I promise you, sir, they are more than capable of guarding one bound-up bird."

A long thick blob of green ooze dropped to the ground and landed with a hiss as Hillmaken spoke. "What news, then?"

"Sir, I have one of the hares—one foretold of in the prophecy."

"Hare?"

"The vultch captured it."

"A *hare* of prophecy, not bear?" Hillmaken whispered to himself in disbelief. He had long believed any prophecy to destroy the Venom Stone would come from a powerful creature, not a lowly shrub-eating pest.

Bazzering continued, "This hare is not common. It is wearing some kind of pack across its back, and it also carries a reed."

Hillmaken's mind was still racing. "Hares?"

"And sir, it *knows* the owl."

"Of course."

"Does this news please you, my lord?"

"Indeed. The vultch has finally proved useful in capturing an enemy, maybe a very important enemy."

"My lord?" Bazzering's voice melted in disappointment as his high hope for accolades came crashing down.

"You—you are lucky I do not demote or imprison you for abandoning your post!"

"I wanted to share this important news personally, in the event we needed to change our plans."

"You seek my favor, and you came to take credit for the work of the vultch."

"Hillmaken, my master. I serve you and the Venom Stone only. My sole intent was to inform you of this early victory."

Hillmaken no longer held back his rage. "We have won nothing yet! *You* are fortunate. There is too much at stake, and we are too close to our end game to make changes in command now. Your ambition must stay in check, Bazzering."

"Yes, my lord."

"Your prisoners will know details of our enemy's plans. Leave now. Find out what is in their little heads. Make them talk by *any* means possible. Then send your messengers back with whatever info you can break out of them. Messengers, not *you*!"

"Yes, Hillmaken."

"You will bring the prisoners with you on your morning march to the Great Lake. I will prepare the ground for the stone."

"Yes, my lord. I will ensure your troops are ready for tomorrow's battle. I will bring the owl and hare."

"A hare?" Eelion hissed as he silently slithered his way into the camp.

"Commander Eelion?" Hillmaken was taken aback at the sight of the giant snake, who had severe injuries across much of his body and was missing an eye.

"*Hares* did this to me! I want revenge. I want them dead," he hissed and then coiled up in front of Hillmaken.

Danix could not hide his excitement as he giggled. "*Hares* did that to *you*?"

Eelion glared at the scorpion with his remaining eye, and his rattle began to pop. Then he hissed again, "Yes, hares."

"Enough!" Hillmaken roared, wanting to stop the inevitable bickering between his lieutenants. "Bazzering was just leaving to tend to his troops. Eelion, you and I will discuss what you saw."

"I will see you tomorrow in victory on the battlefield, Lord Hillmaken," Bazzering said. He did not wait for a reply before disappearing into the night sky.

Hillmaken faced Eelion, still in disbelief that his most loyal and fierce ally was so greatly wounded. This was concerning.

"Hares did this to you, not bears?"

"Yes, hares—the hares foretold in prophecy of the Old Poem, my lord. It must be. They slayed many of my yote fighters and—"

"They slew your yotes? Hares did that?"

"Yes, Hillmaken. They had powers, magic of some kind. They attacked us with fire and rock, and they escaped Mount Flagg by flying."

"Magic? Flying?" Hillmaken snapped.

Eelion slowly rolled backed away from Hillmaken. "Yes, three hares and a shell flew from Mount Flagg with the Oonakestree."

"A *shell?*"

Eelion continued his slow distancing from his irate leader. "Yes, Hillmaken."

"Honu is still sticking his nose into our plans."

Eelion's rattle came alive. "Yes, it was his son's shell that they carried and flew with, sir."

Hillmaken snorted and huffed as his mind tried to process the idea of flying hares. "Wait! This is actually good fortune, Eelion. We have one of the prophesied creatures at Bazzering's camp. If they are what the poem speaks of, their power comes from their unity and…"

"Sir?"

"The hare—it must be *killed*, not questioned." Hillmaken tilted his head back and let out a rolling hiss.

A large dragonfly appeared from the night sky and landed between Eelion and Hillmaken. Its wings twitched in anticipation.

"My messenger, go to our southern base and tell Bazzering to *kill* both of his prisoners. Kill—there will be no questioning. Tell him to bring the trophy of both of their dead bodies on tomorrow's march. I don't care what they know; they must be *destroyed*. Go. He is not far ahead of you."

The dragonfly clicked its acknowledgment before flying away into the night. Hillmaken was still looking upward when a small gray bat fell out of the sky and landed harshly next to him.

It looked up and spoke in pain. "I have seen the two hares and a shell."

"Where? When?" Hillmaken snorted.

"I saw them last as they were north of Honu's canyon." The bat collapsed and died.

Hillmaken turned away from the bat and delivered orders to the great rattler. "Eelion, you are my most trusted. You must go get the Oonakestree back. Bring whatever is left of your yotes. You can trap them in the Slot, where the walls are too steep for any escape."

"Sir, what about the morning plans? I was to lead this division for you while you prepared for the ceremony."

"Our plans have changed only slightly. *I* will lead your division straight to the beach at sunrise. Bazzering will lead his crawlers from the southern camp, and the flyers will join the fight through the Roos Canyon."

Eelion replied, "Yes, Hillmaken. I do as you command."

"Do not kill Honu. Bring him to me so he can witness the rise of the new desert."

"And the two other hares?"

"They are yours; do as you please. Go."

Eelion acknowledged his orders and then slithered away with vengeance on his mind. His rattling tail called out across the expanse to gather the last of his poisonous pack.

Twenty-Six

Olivia had been flying with Sam in tow for over an hour, fortunately with no signs of attacking swarms. He wasn't particularly heavy, but she was exhausted, especially after days filled with running, getting kidnapped, and bug surfing. Fortunately, their destination was getting close.

"Where are we going, Olivia?"

"To the Venom flyers' stronghold. I need to be there at sunrise, which is when they will attack."

"What?"

"While you and your brothers were saving the Oonakestree, other plans were made. Thankfully, you saved me!"

"But, Olivia, what can *we* do against their flyers? There will be millions of them—maybe millions and millions of them."

"Almost there."

"Where?"

"There!" she answered and dropped into a steep dive toward a tight patch of towering saguaros.

"Olivia!" Sam pulled his legs in close as they descended.

She did not respond but continued to dive down toward the biggest of the cacti, a giant with five enormous arms with perfect white flowers blooming across its crown. Sam closed his eyes as they closed in on the spiky giant. Olivia pulled up and spread her wings and let go of his pack, sending him flipping in the air toward the towering plant. Her aim was true, and Sam whizzed safely through an opening of the cactus, where he landed in a tumble and safely came to rest on the back side of the soft interior wall.

Olivia flew in with his reed. "Are you OK?" she asked and turned back around to look outside of the cactus, hoping not to hear or see anything that followed them.

"Yeah, I'm fine. But a heads-up would've been good."

"I'm sorry. I thought I heard a swarm, and I wanted to get you in safely. Are you sure you're OK?"

"Yes, I am fine. I am wondering if you are. You think you can take on millions of Venom flyers."

She smiled and turned back toward the opening and flew out. "Be right back."

"Wait!" Sam said as he gathered himself and hopped over to the cactus window. "Olivia, where did you—"

Before he could finish, Olivia flew back in with two large saguaro fruit, one in each of her talons.

"We need to eat," she said, flinging one of the fruit over to him.

"Thank you." He smiled and immediately tore into the fruit.

Another piece of fruit tumbled in at his feet. Olivia had already gone for seconds. His paws and cheeks were pink from eating the sweet fruit. He immediately felt reenergized.

"Why are we here? Shouldn't we find Honu or King Aridin?"

"Aridin sent me," she assured him. "The Venom Ones have built hundreds of hives in the Roos Canyon among a group of giant oaks that grow along the river."

"Olivia, behind you!" Sam yelled and grabbed her right wing to pull her away from the opening, where four long hairy spider legs had curled up over the edge. He grabbed his reed and jumped toward the opening, ready to fight.

"Sam, wait!" she chirped.

A soft voice whispered up from the opening. "Olivia, it's me, Katlina. Aridin sent me."

"Olivia?" Sam asked and did not take his eyes off the spider legs.

"It's OK, Sam. She is with us. Come in, Kat!"

Sam lowered his reed and stepped back toward Olivia as the spider crawled into the cactus. She was dark brown and covered with fine hairs, and she was bigger than both of them.

"Are you sure?" Sam whispered.

Olivia stepped out to greet the spider. "Katlina is our friend, Sam."

"Yes, Sam, we are allies in the fight for peace in the Desert Realm. Long ago, my great father, along with Aridin and the Elders, rejected a life dedicated to Venom. He committed his allegiance to the way of the light, and the spiders of his line will honor that vow today."

"Sunrise is just hours away. Are you ready?" Olivia asked.

"Yes, we weavers are ready. Those who fly with Venom will not make it to the beach!"

"What is she talking about, Olivia?" Sam asked as he turned to her.

"Olivia is going to lead the Venom flyers into our traps. She was selected by Aridin himself."

"Lead them into the traps? You're going to be bait for them?"

"She will have safe passage. I promise you she will be fine. She is like smoke when she flies. They will not catch her."

"Look for me at sunrise. You will hear us coming," Olivia replied.

"Remember, your path will be marked by a single dot of the morning light," Katlina said as she scuttled backward out of the giant cactus.

Olivia walked to the opening and looked down to see her silently crawl down the sharp spines and back into the desert.

Sam stepped next to her as his ears rotated around, searching for the buzzing threat of swarms.

"Do you hear anything, Sam?"

"Yes, a *very* large swarm. And it's not far from here."

"Good. Those are the hives you hear. That's where I must go."

"You still shouldn't fly."

"I will be fine. You heard Katlina. I am like smoke in the night." She smiled at how silly it sounded.

"It's dangerous, Olivia, and we almost lost you once. I will go with you to make sure you get there safely."

She knew that he was not going to let her go alone and decided to not argue with him. He was probably right: like smoke or not, flying was still dangerous, especially with the swarms so close.

"OK, Sam. Let's go."

"Yes!" Sam responded with a smile. He jumped right out.

"Sam, wait for me," Olivia shouted as she dropped down after him. She snatched him up by his pack and, with a flap of her wings, lowered him safely to the ground.

He stowed his reed back into his pack. "That's all the flying for you until tomorrow. Hop on."

Olivia jumped up on the perch of his reed, and Sam began walking toward the sound of the buzzing of the hives.

Twenty-Seven

The choruses of bugs began their nightly serenades as Nick and Cade continued their quiet march to Honu's. Neither of them said much as they walked across the desert; they only shared concerned glances, for they were still in shock after seeing Sam taken away. Their path had brought them closer to Honu's canyon, as evidenced by the increasing number of boulders and familiar-looking green trees that grew out of the desert.

"Once we bring the Oonakestree to Honu, he will help us find Sam. Once the Oonakestree is safe, the birds are free to fly again, and they will help too." Nick tried to sound confident and reassure his younger brother, although inside, he was just as scared at the thought of losing Sam.

"I hope so. We have to find him—we have to save him!" Cade did not hide the concern in his voice. "The Venomous Ones took our parents from us, and now they have taken away our brother!"

From behind them came a familiar voice. "We will find Sam."

They stopped walking and turned to look behind them. "Honu!" Cade shouted.

Their tracks reflected in the moonlight and revealed that Honu had been walking behind them for some time.

"You have done well, young ones. You have rescued the Oonakestree."

"What about Sam?" Cade replied without acknowledgment of the praise.

"We are searching for him as we speak, and we will find him. Word that you rescued the Oonakestree has already begun to spread; your bravery has brought hope to the Desert Realm."

"Does this mean we've defeated the Venomous Ones? Will they accept peace now?" Nick asked.

"They do not believe in peace anymore, only Venom—Venom or death. They still mean to take over the desert, with or without the prince."

"How can we stop them?" Cade asked. He knew that saving Sam and the desert were one and the same task.

"Honu, will the king and queen be at your den when we bring them the Oonakestree?" Nick asked.

"We are not going to my home. Our enemy is expecting that and lays in wait for us there. We are going to hide the Oonakestree where the prince will stay safe until he is born, which I sense will be very soon."

Honu turned north and began to walk at a pace that surprised both Nick and Cade; they had to run to catch up with him. After several hours of roving across the desert, Honu slowed his pace as they approached a tall, narrow canyon known as the Slot. Ages ago, the raging waters of a fast and powerful river had carved through ancient mountains of red stone. They had left high, smooth walls where now nothing grew. This canyon had long been regarded as a sacred place by most creatures of the Desert Realm. Some believed the walls had the ability to move. The boys' mother, Cari, had told them fantastic stories of the Slot and had promised to take them there. Unfortunately, that day had never come.

"It's beautiful!" Nick gasped.

Honu nodded in agreement and stepped into the canyon. Beams of moonlight bounced around the high, curving walls and lit up a path ahead of them. The sandy ground of the Slot was cool and damp and felt good on their worn-out paws. They followed Honu deeper into twisting shadows. He finally stopped when they stepped into an open pocket of the canyon. A full moon was directly over them.

A soft voice whispered from the shadows. "Honu." It was Sparra.

"My queen, it is so good to see you again," Honu said as he bowed.

"Yes, your remedies cured me. Thank you."

"Praise the light!" Honu replied.

"Do you have my son?"

"Yes, my queen. These are the brave young hares whom the Old Poem promised; they have rescued your prince."

Sparra stepped out of the shadows of the canyon into the moonlight and addressed Nick and Cade. "Thank you.

You have saved my child and rescued the Desert Realm. Your bravery will be rewarded."

"We just want our brother back," Cade said, trying to sound respectful.

"Many are searching for him now. A bat has reported he was last seen with an owl not far from here."

"Olivia!" Nick exclaimed.

"We must hide the Oonakestree with the queen. *Then* we will help in the search," Honu said. Despite saving the prince, he knew they were far from safe, and the war was far from won.

Sparra stepped into the middle of the opening. She spread her wings; tilted her head up to the sky; and let out two long, piercing cries that startled Nick and Cade. The soft sand around their toes began to move, and the rocky walls around them trembled. With another cry from the queen, the wall she was facing split open as if on a seam. It moved apart to reveal a hollow chamber with a nest inside.

Nick and Cade stood in awe, amazed by the shifting walls of stone.

"OK, boys," Honu prompted.

Nick and Cade squatted, unhooked themselves from the reeds, and backed away. Sparra took a step toward them, and Zona's shell opened. Tears of joy and relief ran down her cheeks as she gazed upon the speckled egg.

A high-pitched echo ripped through the Slot. *"Aaaaaaaooooooooow!"*

Honu's head snapped around to the noise, but he calmly said, "Eelion's Venom coyotes…and likely Eelion himself."

He turned back to Nick. "Nick, did you get what Avery asked you to take?"

"Yes."

"Good." Honu smiled. "Now let's move the prince."

"Hurry!" Cade urged.

The pack was closing in on them. Their howling grew louder.

Honu turned to Sparra and assured her, "Hide your son. Do not be afraid; we will not let the desert fall to them."

"Aaaaooooowwwaaaooww!" High-pitched howls echoed all around them.

Cade saw dozens of green eyes sprinting toward them. He leaned over to Nick. "We beat them once; we can beat them now."

Honu kept his eyes on Sparra. "You must go, my queen."

Sparra let out another long call, and the canyon walls closed together, hiding her and the Oonakestree inside.

"Thank you, Honu," Sparra offered.

She let out another screech, and the wall sealed up completely, with no mark to indicate it had ever been separated.

"Aaaaoooooooowww."

"Nick, Cade, secure the shell. We need to move."

"We can fight with you, Honu. We can use our reeds."

A voice materialized from the shadows. "Yes, Honu. Why don't you let the little rodents fight me?" Eelion hissed as he emerged from around a corner of the Slot.

Honu responded, "It looks like you lost the last time. Maybe I *should* let them fight you again."

"Trickery and magic, Honu! How else could weak little hares defeat me and my yotes? It is of no consequence now. The final battle will begin in hours, and you and your kind will fall."

The last of his pack arrived in the Slot and surrounded the trio from every angle. There were too many of them to fight and no way out.

Honu lowered his head and uttered, "We surrender, Eelion."

Nick and Cade exchanged a concerned glance before Nick objected. "Honu, we can't give up—not now."

Honu ignored Nick's plea as he addressed Eelion. "We will surrender…but *only* to Hillmaken."

"Maybe you have grown wise, Honu. Maybe you finally understand that the Venom is the true power that will rule the desert."

"Take me to Hillmaken. I will open my son's shell for him, but only if you spare these young ones. What you *stole* is inside the shell. Your master will be pleased with you, Eelion."

"Yes, the Oonakestree—safely tucked away in *your son's* shell. Zona, wasn't it?" He hissed with a sick smile, wanting to hurt Honu. Eelion had been there the day Zona had died, and he knew all too well the details surrounding the young tortoise's death.

"Yes, it is the shell of my son."

Eelion's grin widened with delight, and his rattle came to life. This stirred his yotes; several of them strained their necks skyward and howled.

"Yes, my beloved Venom yotes, lead the way for our prisoners! We march toward our destiny—our victory." Eelion laughed, causing several of his wounds to crack open and ooze.

His rattle stopped, and his yotes funneled into a narrow channel, the path that led out of the Slot and to the Great Lake. Honu nodded silent assurance to the questioning faces of Nick and Cade. Then all three fell in line with Eelion's marching pack.

Twenty-Eight

Hillmaken's dragonfly messenger caught up with Bazzering just minutes away from their southern base of operations. It clicked out Hillmaken's orders just as the camp came into view.

"Kill them, huh?" Bazzering answered with a slow smile.

More clicks from the messenger, but this time, Bazzering did not respond, and the grin disappeared from his face. His focus shifted to the moonlit camp—*his* camp—below them, and something was wrong. The sleeping mounds of resting soldiers he had left just hours ago were no more. Instead, dead snakes, lizards, and other Venom creepers were scattered in pieces all across the camp. The Venom Stone pulsed in the center of the base, emitting a misty green light.

Bazzering and the dragonfly landed and assessed the carnage. There was slow movement by the few remaining survivors around the edges of the camp, but overall, the base was still. When Bazzering saw his lieutenant lying motionless on the ground, he flew over to him and kicked him in his midsection.

"Attacked?" He bent down and shouted into his face, "Who did this?"

One of the spiders who had chased Sam dropped down from a nearby cactus and replied, "The Venom Stone did this."

"Who?"

"The stone, sir."

"The stone?" More shock ran across Bazzering's face. "Where are the prisoners?"

"They escaped."

"Escaped? No!"

The spider continued, "The Venom Stone began to pulse as the prisoners flew off, as if it was angered by their escape. The pulsing awoke the scaled ones first, and they just began attacking and tearing one another apart. Their own kind, sir. Then the centipedes and the scorpions joined in the chaos. I think the stone told them to."

Bazzering scanned the aftermath of the melee. "I have no army to bring to Hillmaken. I am doomed!"

"You still have all of us spiders, most of the ants, and quite a few scorpions, sir. We spiders knew better than to fight among ourselves."

"Doomed." Bazzering stared up into the stars.

"Sir, you can gather the survivors who fled the fight, and us eight-leggers will secure the stone for transport."

"Doomed."

"Sir!"

Bazzering snapped his head back down to the spider. "Yes, you are correct. Mobilize the crawlers, and secure the stone for transport. Daybreak is coming soon, and I—*we*—must deliver the Venom Stone to Hillmaken."

"Yes, sir."

"Perhaps he will spare us."

The spider made no reply but turned and belted out several long, rolling clicks. Thousands of spiders appeared from the darkness. They came from everywhere: circling on webs down from the cacti, emerging from nearby shrubs, and springing out from their makeshift trapdoors. They scurried toward the middle of the camp, crawling over their fallen comrades. Thick, fast lines of ants poured out of mounds all through the camp, while shiny black scorpions popped out of the sand—all while the Venom Stone continued its slow, steady pulse. The army of insects gathered and closed in around the stone and then froze in a collective daze, awestruck by its dark beauty, absorbing the evil power it emitted.

"Prepare the stone!" Bazzering yelled to the remaining troops.

His shrill order snapped the insects out of their trance, scattering them in all directions. The spiders quickly began weaving webs around the stone, while the other insects went to gather the survivors.

Bazzering continued to circle around the base, weighing the brutality his own troops had inflicted on themselves. He still held hope that Hillmaken would spare him in the morning. Although he would be bringing only a fraction of his army to the Great Lake, at least he would have the Venom Stone. He continued his supervision of the new carrier; the spiders used ocotillo branches and webs to build the new transport system. They would be marching soon.

Twenty-Nine

Hillmaken startled his slumbering troops awake with a resounding roar that tore through his camp like a thunderclap. He hissed again, and his troops organized into lines, separating and gathering up into groups of their own kind. Spiders, lizards, and snakes made up the bulk of this force, although several of Hillmaken's war-pig experiments snorted and roamed the perimeter of the camp.

"Get in formation. We march now!"

Yellow jackets and wasps zoomed across the camp and delivered Hillmaken's orders to the thousands of slow-moving soldiers who were still trying wake up and shake off the cool air.

"Now!"

Poison sprayed from Hillmaken's mouth as he raged. There was no time for any kind of delay. The entirety of the camp jumped at his bellow and started their march across the desert. Lizards made up the first row of fighters in his battle formation. Behind them, the snakes formed the second row, their rattled tails silenced as they awaited orders. The two rows of reptiles were followed by a long, uninterrupted row of spiders of all shapes and sizes.

The troops continued to fall in, with alternating and expanding rows of reptiles and insects, until they created a large triangle behind Hillmaken. The havelin continued to roam around the fringes but did not join the formation.

"Well done, my Venom fighters. Soon, the morning sun will rise and warm your blood. Today, we march to our destiny!"

His army erupted with popping rattles, shrill hisses, and snapping fangs. Hillmaken grinned as he looked out across his glorious band of warriors. He sensed his victory was imminent.

"For too long, our ways have been pushed aside, but no more. You have all chosen the powerful and *true* way. Today, Venom will rule the desert!"

Hillmaken's followers again responded with a raucous show of adoration and approval, and he basked in their praise for several moments. He silenced his loyal subjects with another rolling roar and then spun around and led his army to the Great Lake.

▲ ▲ ▲

Sam carefully made his way through the cacti-covered rolling desert that led to the oak-filled start of the canyon. Olivia was still balanced on top of the reed and scanned the skies as they made their way.

"It's too quiet—no bugs, no birds, no bats, nothing," Sam said to his passenger.

"I think the desert is holding its breath, getting ready for the day that is coming."

Sam slowed down to a walk. "I smell the river, and I can feel the buzzing."

"I feel it too. We need to get as close as we can to the old trees without being seen. When the sun rises, our plan begins. There is a bluff where we will hide and wait."

Sam nodded and said, "Get low; we are getting close."

Olivia leaned forward until her head rested on top of Sam's, just between his ears. She spread her wings and wrapped them completely around him, hiding him as they made their way up the rise that overlooked the canyon and the fast-moving waters of the Roos. For eons, snow from the Calaas had melted down the mountains to form the Roos, which had eventually carved its way through the desert to become the main water source of the Great Lake.

Across the river they saw a group of remarkably large oak trees that had grown near, around, and out of the soft banks. These ancient trees marked the beginning of the canyon. Hundreds of giant paper hives hung from their long sturdy branches.

Sam hopped up the last twisting slopes of the hill and stopped in front of a sprawling ironwood tree that grew near the edge of the steep wall. Olivia jumped down from her perch, and they both stepped under the tree's branches.

"I hope Nick and Cade made it to Honu," Sam said as he stared at the giant trees, which were alive with activity.

Olivia leaned over and wrapped her wing around him, covering his sensitive ears from the dull buzz of the swarm. "Have faith, Sam. After all, your capture ended up saving me."

They would stay huddled together as they waited for sunrise.

Thirty

Eelion continued to taunt Honu as he and his yotes marched them through the Slot toward the Great Lake. He reminded him who again had the Oonakestree and how he and his long-eared friends would soon bow Hillmaken and follow the way of the Venom.

Honu made no reply and showed no emotion to the hateful words Eelion poured on them during their trek. However, Nick and Cade had to fight back tears and the urge to speak out to defend their friend.

Honu could see the anguish in their eyes and whispered encouragement to them. "Do not listen to what Eelion says. Do not be afraid of him or his words."

Eelion's tail came alive, and he whirled to face them. "Did you say something, Honu?" he hissed. His rattle shook at a dizzying rate.

"Yes, I told them not to listen to the evil you spit from your mouth."

"Evil? Evil is all perspective, Honu. *We* think *you* are evil for rejecting the gift of the stone, the gift that fell from the heavens, the gift meant for all." Eelion's tongue darted in and out, and his blood began to boil.

"The Venom Stone distorts the truth. It is a curse, not a gift. And now you are evil too. I remember who you *were*, Eelion," Honu replied.

"Enough!" Eelion's tail stopped as he spun back around and slithered ahead of his pack.

Honu's strength and calm were inspiring. Nick and Cade felt fear ease its grip on them. Despite being captured and surrounded by dozens of Eelion's yotes, they suddenly felt at ease.

"Where did Eelion go?" Nick asked.

"Ahead to the Gathering Beach; he wants to see Hillmaken first so he can announce the arrival of his prizes—the Oonakestree and us."

Cade echoed Honu with a sly smile. "The Oonakestree."

"Yes, the Oonakestree," Nick added.

Thirty-One

The Elders arrived at the Gathering Beach, just as they had done when Honu had brought them together to share the news of the attack and the kidnapping. Throughout the night, wise and ancient leaders had walked, crawled, and slithered from every corner of the Desert Realm to be at the Great Lake. Other than the hummingbirds, who still flew undetected, all other birds rode on the antlers, shells, and backs of their traveling allies.

They assembled on the beach and encircled Aridin, their king. The smallest creatures stood closest to him while the larger animals like wolves, horses, and rams made up the outer edges. Most had only heard of the attack on Aridin; few had seen him since his wing had been viciously removed by Eelion's band of frogs. It pained them all to see their great king this way, but he showed no fear and stood strong and tall as he spoke to them.

"Hillmaken is almost here. You can smell him and his vile army as they approach. Soon, the Venomous Ones will be on this beach, and they plan to destroy us if we do not accept and choose their way. But we will stand together in unity, and we will fight them. We will not let the Desert Realm fall to their evil ways."

A loud screech echoed out of the sky; it was the vultch. Hillmaken's flying monstrosity circled over them several times before it swooped down toward the Gathering Beach. Its talons just missed the top of Aridin's head; the king did not move or flinch from the attacker. The vultch circled one more time and then let out another long and terrifying screech before it landed on a narrow, twisting bluff near the beach.

"Pay no mind to that flying abomination," Aridin continued. "He is cruel and corrupt, like the rest who blindly follow the call of that cursed stone."

A sliver of the new day's sun edged its way up out of the flat horizon, lighting up the Elders with a soft, warm glow. The moment of serenity and peace was torn apart by Hillmaken, who snarled and growled as he clawed his way across the beach. His grand army followed him.

"The Venom Stone brings power to those who follow it. You know that, Aridin. Let me show you."

Aridin said nothing.

"Prepare the beach!" Hillmaken screamed his orders.

Aridin and the Elders silently watched as hundreds of lizards broke formation and scurried across the white sands toward the waterline. They stopped at the edge of the beach, where the Roos River fed into the Grand Lake, and began to dig a channel in the sand. Hillmaken hissed his approval.

The circle of the Elders opened up, and Aridin stepped out and walked across the beach toward Hillmaken.

"It doesn't have to end this way. Innocent lives will be lost in this senseless fight."

"Then don't fight, Aridin. Accept the Venom Stone. You will become a truly *great* king, a king who sacrificed himself for his kingdom. A sacrifice for the good of all."

"I have seen how your beloved stone corrupts. We want nothing of it."

"Not corruption, Aridin. The Venom Stone gives strength and clarity, and you lack both. I do not need *you* to rule the desert skies; your *son* will."

"Your words convict you, Hillmaken. Your vision is clouded. The stone rules by fear, not strength."

The two leaders stood in the sand, now just feet apart, with their eyes locked on to each other. The Venom army squirmed with excitement as the sun's warmth spread across their formation. Hillmaken turned away from Aridin toward something buzzing and circling above him. It was Bazzering.

"Hillmaken, my troops—*your* troops—will be here momentarily."

"With the stone?" Hillmaken questioned.

"Yes, sir. The spiders have the Venom Stone."

Hillmaken saw a small army of spiders towing the Venom Stone behind them in a suspended blob of branches and webs.

"Spiders?" Hillmaken faced the incompetent creature. "Lizards are in charge of the transport of the Venom Stone!"

Bazzering landed but did not raise his eyes to Hillmaken as he continued. "Sir, we lost many of the scaled ones last night."

Hillmaken's eye widened. "Scaled ones, lost? How?"

"My master, when the prisoners escaped, the stone reacted and—"

"Escaped?"

"Yes, Hillmaken, my leader. The guards I left in charge reported that the Venom Stone became angered and began to glow with an intensity they had never seen before. Its power overtook the camp. Your soldiers became crazed and violently turned against one another."

"You let the prisoners escape? The very same prisoners you came to gloat about last night?"

The rage festering deep within Hillmaken boiled over, and his ire was now focused on his incompetent soldier. The lizard did not wait for the cowering wasp's reply. Instead, he took a step toward his lieutenant, raised his right claw, and squashed the life out of him. Bazzering's grand plans were snuffed out on the sandy beach. Hillmaken turned back to Aridin and let out a piercing roar.

Thirty-Two

Hillmaken's call echoed through the rocky walls of the Roos Canyon. The circling swarms heeded their master's call to assemble. Sam and Olivia watched as the wasps, hornets, and yellow jackets poured down from the skies and out of the hives and amassed together around the trees. There were so many of them.

"Did you hear that?" Sam whispered. "I think that was their signal."

"Yes, that's my signal, too."

"Please, be careful."

"I will, Sam. Thank you again for saving me. You are *my* hero."

She kissed the top of his head and flew out from under the cover of the tree over the river, straight toward the giant swarm of swirling insects.

"Follow the light!" Sam reminded Olivia with a heavy heart. He marveled again at her bravery and hoped this would not be the last time he saw her.

Thirty-Three

Reflections of the new day's sun danced across the serene waters of the Great Lake.

The news of lost troops before any battle had stoked Hillmaken's rage white hot, causing slow green poison to seep from pores atop his back. With hatred in his eyes, he turned back to face the Elders and was about to speak when a long-legged, spindly spider appeared on the beach and fearfully approached him.

"Hillmaken, sir, we have the Venom Stone."

Hillmaken paused as the words traveled slowly through his mind, finally taking hold when the spider spoke again.

"Well done, spider." Hillmaken turned to Aridin and added, "You see how venomous spiders obey me and the stone? Where are your armies of eight-legged warriors?"

Aridin said nothing.

Hillmaken turned away and addressed the spider again. "Take the Venom Stone to my lizards who are finishing the construction of the pool." He looked up the beach. "It is where the river meets the lake."

Aridin kept his eyes locked on Hillmaken. "You will find no converts here."

Hillmaken snapped back at him. "Some *will* choose the way of Venom. When they are faced with their own deaths or, more importantly, the deaths of those they love, some *will* convert."

"You are wrong in so many ways. This stone you worship has destroyed you. It changed you from what you were."

"I could kill you right now, Aridin. However, I want you to witness the demise of your kingdom, the fall of the followers of the light, and most importantly, the conversion of *your* son."

Aridin held back the overpowering urge to leap up and tear the lizard apart for all he had done and all he planned to do. Nevertheless, he suppressed his anger and spoke calmly. "We would rather face death than live a life infected by that stone."

"Yes, I know most will not convert today; that is *really* what this is all about. That is why this new pool will be permanent. Soon, water from the Roos will drink up the stone's power before I route it back into the Great Lake. I will create a new source of life for the desert, a Venom Lake. A gift all can partake in."

"You will have to kill all of us for your plans to succeed." Aridin stepped even closer to Hillmaken.

A laugh rose from the southern end of the beach; it was Eelion. "I would be happy to finish the job I started, Aridin."

Honu, Nick, and Cade remained silent as Eelion paraded them up the beach past the Elders. Aridin and Honu exchanged a quick glance as they passed.

One of Eelion's yotes stopped walking, tilted its head back, and let out a whistling howl that was quickly echoed by the dozens of others that surrounded them. They could smell the stone and the tension of the standoff.

Eelion coiled up on the beach and jeered at Aridin and the Elders as he hissed, "I believe you all know my prisoners and the shell they tote with them." He turned back to his leader. "You know what is inside, Lord Hillmaken?"

He nodded. "Yes."

Eelion continued, "We again have the Oonakestree, Hillmaken. We have our new prince."

Hillmaken's mouth broke open in a wet, gruesome smile that revealed the uneven rows of his jagged and misplaced teeth. He enjoyed seeing Honu as a prisoner.

"Yes, Eelion, the *new* prince. The prince the Desert Realm deserves!"

He maintained his sinister grin as he marched up the beach toward his newly constructed conversion pool. He began to believe that despite Bazzering's stupendous failings, his plan still might work. Aridin, Honu, and the Elders were in his capture, along with two of the so-called saviors of the Old Poem. Most importantly, he again had the Oonakestree.

This was the biggest pool Hillmaken had ever commanded to be built. It sloped down and was deep enough to hold enough water for even the largest of the desert converts. Two twisting channels were dug on either end of the pool: one where water flowed in from the river, the other flowing back into the Great Lake. He paced around the pool and inspected the work of his lizards, and he was pleased. The steady flow of the river had already filled the pool and started its slow green flow back into the lake. The Venom Stone now rested upright, partly submerged in pocket of sand in the shallow end of the pool. The water had already started its green glow, as small bubbles popped up across the surface.

Now that Hillmaken was satisfied with the construction, he turned and roared out his order. "It is time!"

Thirty-Four

S am's grip tightened on his reed as he stood under the branches of the ironwood. He watched Olivia fly directly toward the staggering swarms that now circled around the oaks. The morning sunlight reflected off her with flashes of white and gray as she flew; she did look like smoke.

Sam marveled at her grace and her profound courage and whispered to himself, "Please, please, please, let her be OK." He squinted, and his ears fell back flat on his head; it was getting hard to watch.

Olivia swooped into the edge of the swarm and speared two flyers with her long, sharp talons. The death cry from the two wasps alerted the entire swarm, and they soon focused their collective attention on her. Their simple brains forgot about waiting for Hillmaken's second order, the one that would signal the start of their flight. They only saw a bird, and they all wanted to kill it.

Sam could sense the change in the swarm and yelled out, "Go now, Olivia!"

She let go of the two dead bugs and did a tight flip and descended straight down toward the river.

"Go, go, go!" Sam yelled as he stepped out from under the tree into the morning light.

He watched as Olivia gained speed in her descent into the canyon, keeping just ahead of the entire swarm that now hunted her. She pulled up from her dive just above the surface of the river. The closest of her pursuers could not navigate the change in time and splashed into the river. Thousands of the swarm drowned because of Olivia's quick turn, but millions more still chased her.

Thirty-Five

E elion's yotes yipped as they circled around the Elders, herding them toward Hillmaken's new and glorious conversion pool.

Honu silently marched, staring out on the Great Lake, where the sun's reflection had risen full and bounced across its dark water. The damp sand reminded him of the morning walks he and Zona had had on this very beach. His son would always pose thoughtful questions about the mysteries of their desert and other realms of the earth. Zona's inquiries always ended with even bigger questions about the worlds that existed in the Realm of the Stars.

"Honu? Honu, where are you, old friend? You seem a million miles away."

"I am here, Hillmaken," he replied, but his mind was still on those days with Zona, and his eyes were still locked on the lake.

"I am so glad you Elders are *all* here—all here with your king." Hillmaken snarled at them. "You rejecters will all bear witness to the birth of the *new* desert!"

Eelion slid closer to Honu and hissed, "Why do you not fight? Here are the great Elders of the Desert Realm, but

161

you stand here like fools on this beach awaiting your doom. Where are your armies? Are you going to just give up?"

Hillmaken answered for them. "Yes, Eelion, they have given up. They know they have been defeated by Venom. Their feathered ones are grounded, and the Elders stand in front of us unprotected." He turned his head upward. "No flyers came to fight. They have given up. We have won!"

A low buzz arose like a faint echo from across the lake. The sound stopped Hillmaken's victory declaration.

Eelion's joy could not be contained. "Hillmaken, my lord, I hear our deadly flyers coming from the Roos Canyon. They will be with us soon."

"Ah, yes. Elders, do you hear that sound? It's the sound of the *new* sky coming to welcome you to the world of Venom and to celebrate their new prince."

Hillmaken coughed up several deep, wet laughs. His plan was working.

Eelion's rattle snapped alive as he shifted the focus of his remaining eye back to Nick and Cade. He ordered, "Bring the Oonakestree to the pool. You two pitiful creatures have the honor of carrying the prince to his glorious conversion. Maybe he will show favor upon you and your pathetic kind."

Eelion's yotes again began to yip and howl as they ushered Cade and Nick to the pool.

Honu spoke to them. "Don't be afraid."

Eelion's tail grew louder. He gloated: "No, Honu, they should be very afraid."

Thirty-Six

Olivia cut through the cool air of the canyon, flying so close to the river she left a small rolling wake behind her. Although the buzz of the giant swarm grew louder as it pursued her, she heard only Sam's voice in her head, urging her to look for the light. The dark, twisting storm of insects had gained on her and was about to swallow her up.

Hillmaken had questioned Aridin about the absence of spiders loyal to his cause; Olivia was now racing toward that answer. Spiders from every corner of the Desert Realm who had denied the Venom Stone had gathered in the Roos Canyon. With the help of flying insects, hundreds of thousands of spiders had spent the last two days working together to construct a series of enormous canyon-crossing webs. Each web was a sticky transparent trap that spanned wall to wall of the twisting valley. Woven into each tightly knitted curtain of web was a small circular opening no bigger than a hummingbird's egg. The morning sunlight refracted through the tapestry of webs, focusing the rays onto a singular opening that marked Olivia's way through.

The temporary passage was held open by strategically positioned spiders that drew back on several long strands that created the tiny window of light.

Olivia dipped her left wing and cut around a sharp corner of the canyon; then she leveled out and again zoomed over surface of the water. She was heading straight toward the first of the giant webs that Katlina and her clan had stitched together. The swarm was so close she could feel its collective buzz on her tail feathers. The web was strangely translucent as it hung across the canyon like a thin cloud. Olivia thought it looked beautiful. She darted up toward the tiny spot of sunlight that shone near the very center of the first web. Just as her beak broke the plane of light, she tucked her wings in, and the hole was pulled open just wide enough for her to fly safely through. With a clip of their fangs, the spiders cut the strands that held open her window. The opening snapped shut behind her. Only a handful of Venom flyers made it through the web with her; the rest sailed into the sticky trap. The swarm's force pushed straight into the web, stretching it forward until the supporting webs popped off their canyon-wall supports. The long sticky strands snapped around and wrapped up the front wave of the swarm into a giant sticky blob, which dropped into the river.

The swarm continued its crazed pursuit of Olivia and paid no mind to their drowning comrades. The insects followed the bird's every move as she twisted through the air back and forth over the water. Each time she passed through one of the lighted openings, another wave of Hillmaken's flyers got trapped in sticky nets of webs and died in the water.

Thirty-Seven

The morning sun warmed Sam's back as the wind stirred small eddies across his soft coat. He stared down the canyon, hoping and praying his dear friend was safe. The last of the swarm had just disappeared around a bend, and its collective buzz was now a fading echo. His ears swiveled back toward more noise that was coming from the trees. He turned and saw thousands of Venom flyers still circling around the gray paper fortresses.

Most of the swarm was gone, but Sam knew that the hives needed to be destroyed—he would have to somehow break them off the branches. Sam stepped out to the edge of the canyon wall and scanned around for a safe way down to the shores. His quick survey revealed that the fastest way down would be to leap off the towering ledge into the river and then trek back up the shore a short distance to the trees. All other options would require long walks down from the canyon. Still, he did not want to do any more jumping into rivers unless he absolutely had to. He counted the hives as he walked down the incline toward a path that would lead to the river. Just as he counted nineteen, a flash of pain blew up in his right foot. He had stepped squarely onto the sharp end of a jagged stone. He wanted to scream but instead swung his reed down into the face of the toe-smashing rock. It lit up with a thunderous crack and a white-hot flash of light. The stone smoldered and sparked as it soared over the tallest of the oak trees, an arcing plume of white smoke trailing behind it.

"Whoa!" Sam said and then smiled as he looked down at the scattered rocks that lay all around him.

The remaining swarm did not notice the small fireball that screamed over them. They were focused solely on the maintenance of the hives, patching holes and checking up on the next generation of fighters that grew inside.

Sam stepped over to another stone that was slightly bigger than the first and centered himself over it. He lowered his reed until it softly kissed the face of the stone. Then in a blur, he brought it back over his right shoulder and whipped it down into the rock. Like the first stone, this one lit up with an ear-splitting crack and a flash of brilliant light—but unlike the first, this one sailed straight into the middle of one of the trees. It broke apart in a flash of white sparks as it exploded into a branch. The smoldering shards ripped through the closest hives and immediately ignited them.

"Yes!"

He hopped over to an even bigger stone that sat just off the edge of the canyon. He grinned as he swung down on it. The white-hot explosion from the impact temporarily blinded him and blew him back onto his tail. His ears were pinned down in pain; he dropped his reed to rub away the stars that now flashed in his eyes. As the world came back into view, he saw the plumes of gray smoke floating out from the band of trees, and his sensitive nose could already smell it. As he looked across the canyon into the trees, he saw that only the hives were on fire. The thick knotty branches and green leaves of the trees were unharmed by the burning stones. However, the heat quickly ate through the heavy hives' delicate support systems. One by one, they began to snap off the branches and bounce down into the river below, splashing with a hiss and plume of sinking smoke.

"Yes!" Sam shouted again and began to swirl his reed around his head.

The spinning reed created a high-pitched whistle, which caught the attention of the remaining Venom flyers that had poured out of the smoldering hives.

"Uh-oh." Sam stopped the spinning.

As the flyers raced toward him, fear struck him. He realized he would not be able to outrun the stinging swarm, and he knew that his only option was to jump.

Thirty-Eight

Although the far-off sound of the exploding rocks was hidden by the shake of Eelion's rattle and the howl from his yotes, the Elders saw small bursts of light popping in the twists of the Roos Canyon. Hillmaken continued to gloat about his forthcoming victory, which seemed all but assured now, while Danix scuttled around him in excitement.

"Elders of the desert!" Hillmaken roared. This silenced Eelion and his pack, and the beach again was quiet and still. "Elders, today you will bear witness to the glorious birth of the new Venom prince of the desert."

The silence of the Elders again infuriated Eelion, who circled around them and continued to goad them. "Why do you stand here in defeat? It's pathetic!"

"Open the shell," Hillmaken commanded.

Nick and Cade slid their reeds free from the shell and then walked around to stand on either side of Honu.

"Open it!"

"You don't have to do this, Hillmaken," Aridin reminded him.

"You had your chance to rule this realm, but you proved to be too weak. Look at you now. You are a helpless one-winged bird!"

"Yes!" Eelion laughed as he continued his circling of the Elders.

"Open it!" Hillmaken roared again.

Nick and Cade turned and looked at Honu, who nodded to them.

"Hillmaken, look—their flyers!" Danix interrupted as he inched toward his master.

Eelion stopped his circling, coiled up, and looked up in the western sky. "Finally, you show courage and fight."

Hillmaken replied with sarcastic delight. "Yes, Eelion, it looks like they may have some fight in them after all." He turned back to Aridin and continued, "It is an impressive array of flyers, and you don't often see bug and bird flying united. However, my swarm will easily overtake them. Just one sting from my fighters can take out any of your birds. You will lose them all."

The Elders kept their collective focus on the shell and did not look back at the massive swarm that was racing over the lake toward them. Aridin tilted his head upward and let out a powerful call that echoed across the water and startled Eelion out of his coil. The birds of the oncoming swarm returned his call with a collective screech that bounced across off the rocky mesas and mountains that surrounded the Great Lake. The avian reply to Aridin was followed by a deep growing buzz from the millions of insects that flew with them.

Danix sidled closer to Hillmaken. "Where are *our* flyers, Hillmaken? I can't hear them anymore."

"Our army will soon be out of the canyon and will easily overtake them."

"There are so many!" Danix added.

Hillmaken roared, "We still have numbers, you fool! Look at the magnificent army that stands before us now. On my command, they will destroy all who refuse to bow to the new prince."

Eelion slithered up the beach and looked up toward the canyon, waiting for the arrival of the Venom flyers. They should have been out of the canyon by now. Then he saw something.

"Hillmaken?"

"Open up the shell, now!" Poison sprayed from the Venom leader's mouth as he stomped and raged, ignoring Eelion.

"Sir!"

"Open it!"

Honu nodded to Nick and Cade, and they extended their reeds out over the shell. Without a sound, the shell unhinged and began to open.

"Hillmaken, sir, our swarm!" Eelion pleaded to his leader as he continued to stare in the direction of the canyon.

Hillmaken's eyes were locked on the shell, and he did not see the small gray owl flying out of the canyon. However, Eelion, Danix, and the Elders did.

"A bird?" Eelion hissed with sudden concern and then slithered back to Hillmaken.

Eelion's cry broke Hillmaken's fixation on the shell. He too looked up toward the canyon. He expected to see his glorious and deadly swarm racing toward the beach, but instead, he saw a single bird zooming over the still water. The owl was still being chased by the last remaining Venom flyers, the lucky few who had avoided getting snared in the giant webs.

"My swarm?" Hillmaken's confusion turned to rage. "A *bird*? A *bird*?"

Olivia pulled up from the water and soared directly into the oncoming swarm. It opened up around her like a tunnel. Once she was safely in its protection, the swarm snapped shut and collapsed on the last of her pursuers. The beetles, dragonflies, and praying mantises of the swarm joined forces to quickly slay the remainder of Hillmaken's Venom flyers.

Hillmaken turned away from the sight of his aerial defeat and roared again, "Open the shell!"

As the shell opened, the ground began to tremble, and ripples broke out from the beach and dashed across the lake. Hillmaken's eyes grew wide, and he shrank back away from the shell. There was no egg inside, only a small triangular stone, which was suddenly growing.

The Balancing Stone cracked and boomed like a monsoon as it became bigger and expanded upward over the beach. The earth continued to tremble as the stone returned to the size it had been when Nick had first picked it up off the ledge. It now towered into the sky over the beach. The tapered end of the stone fit perfectly into the hollow of Zona's shell, which held true and did not sink into the sand despite the staggering weight that was now pressing down on it.

Hillmaken hissed, "Where is the Oonakestree?"

Aridin replied, "My son, the prince of the desert, is with his mother, the queen. Both are safe, hidden away from you and your plans."

After a moment of confusion, Hillmaken yelled, "*You* are not safe yet!" Then he stormed across the beach straight into the shadow of the Balancing Stone to address his legions.

"Venom fighters, it is time to destroy the followers of the light. The Elders who stand before you have rejected the way of the Venom Stone, and they have deceived us for the last time. Attack without mercy! March to your victory!"

Hillmaken's army reacted with great energy as they slithered and crept out of the desert onto the Gathering Beach. Their triangular formation narrowed up as they converged on the Elders.

As Hillmaken's army plodded ahead, Honu stepped behind the Balancing Stone, laid the crown of his head against it, and pushed. With a snap like twig, the giant rock began to fall. The stone's shadow grew wide and long as it spread across the beach. The entirety of Hillmaken's ground troops were now marching under it.

Eelion, who still sat coiled up near the lake's edge, appeared hypnotized as he stared up into the storm of birds and bugs that were now circling over the Gathering Beach. The screaming, swirling air snapped him out of his stupor. He slithered past the Elders toward Hillmaken but stopped when he saw the impending doom that was falling out of the sky.

"Hillmaken!" he tried to warn. "Hillmaken—the stone!"

The whistling of gravity stopped, and the morning air was ripped away in a deafening vacuum. A moment of hollow silence was replaced by the thunderous impact of the Balancing Stone as it crashed down on the Gathering Beach. Sand exploded in all directions as the stone easily drove into the ground. The impact was so great that all those on the beach were bounced up in the air.

Almost all of Hillmaken's marching troops perished instantaneously under the weight of the Balancing Stone. The few who survived fled in fear, disappearing into the desert. Eelion's yotes yelped and howled, scattering and sprinting in all directions; several ran straight into the lake trying to swim to safety. They didn't make it, though.

▲ ▲ ▲

Hillmaken heard Eelion's warning in time and leaped toward the sunlight, away from the ominous and growing shadow. He was more fortunate than his soldiers, as the Balancing Stone spared his life and took only his tail and the lower half of his right hind leg.

"Hillmaken?" Eelion uttered with panic and concern as he raced toward his master.

"My army. No!" Hillmaken roared, trying to crawl out from under the edge of the Balancing Stone.

Eelion gasped when he saw Hillmaken's injuries. The last remaining pieces of skin and scale tore away from his back and flattened tail. A thick trail of blood dripped from the gash in his severed leg and the nub of exposed tail-bone. Eelion coiled up around his master to protect him. His head swayed back and forth, and his rattle clicked furiously.

Eelion glared at Honu. "You will pay for this!"

Nick and Cade stepped out toward Eelion and brought their reeds back over their shoulders, ready to smash the other eye out of his head.

Honu shook his head to stop their advance. "Not now."

"It is over, Eelion. Look at Hillmaken; he is at death's door," Aridin said.

As Hillmaken spoke, his hatred painfully melted into regret and rue. "I will die, then. I was the first to embrace the Venom Stone. And I rightfully stole it back from you. I converted so many to its way."

"Your flyers have drowned, Hillmaken. Your armies are buried."

"I had your son, Aridin. He would have been *born* of the stone. He would have been blessed with the power of Venom. He would have ruled the skies like no other bird has."

"You have been defeated. Birds have once again take flight in our skies."

"A Venomous bird to rule the desert and beyond it!" Hillmaken roared.

Aridin roared, "It is finished!"

Hillmaken grunted with fading defiance as the reality of his defeat set in and took hold. He surveyed the beach, sniffing the air with several long, deep breaths. His energy was fading. Aridin was right; he was dying. He shifted his gaze down the length of the mammoth stone that had just pulverized his grand army—the stone he had heard stories of growing up but hadn't believed in. Hillmaken then dropped his head in defeat, admitting, "You are right, Aridin. It is finished."

Eelion pleaded with rage at Hillmaken. "No, Master, we cannot give up. *You* cannot give up. I believe in the Venom. I believe in you! Together, we can rebuild our armies again!"

Hillmaken coughed up blood and then tried to speak. "It is over, Eelion. Look around you. The armies we built have been washed away. Our victory has been stolen from us."

"Hillmaken, it is *not* over!" Eelion's pleading turned to rage.

"Washed away…"

Eelion uncoiled himself and leaped into the bubbling water of the conversion pool. He glared at Aridin, snapping viciously and uncontrollably and then wrapped himself around the Venom Stone. His body trembled and tremored while he hissed, as if in great pain. As he absorbed the power of the Venom Stone, he began to grow even larger, and his skin began to change. Large diamond-shaped scales emerged from his sides, pushing out clusters of smaller scales that fell off and dissolved into the water. The new scales were dark but translucent and had a green glow. His rattle popped at a feverish pace, and he continued to flail in the water.

"I feel its strength. It speaks to me, Hillmaken! We can still be victorious!"

"Eelion, enough. It will kill you," Hillmaken warned.

Eelion's head snapped straight upward and then violently slammed down onto the beach. Half of his body was now out of the pool as he lay motionless. The Venom Stone had brought about another change in the giant snake. Three eyes had sprouted from the empty eye socket on the top of his head. Two were identical to his left eye—yellow and reptilian—but the third that was stacked on top of the other two was bulbous and black; it was the eye of a spider.

Cade tightened his grip on his reed and looked at Honu. "Is he dead?"

Before he could get a response, Eelion's head slowly rose up off the beach, and his body unwound from the stone.

"He's alive," Sam whispered.

Eelion's jaw was unhinged and dangled awkwardly, exposing his long, sharp fangs. He hissed at the Elders before collapsing again on the sand with a thud.

"Stay back, boys," Honu warned.

Eelion snapped alive again and began to twist and roll across the beach until he stopped in the shallow waters of the Great Lake's shoreline. The cool water awakened him, and he reformed into a tight coil. He tried to shake the dizziness out of his head; he could not make sense of the strange vision his three new eyes had given him.

"Look at me, Hillmaken. It has given me even *more* power. Don't you see—we can defeat them. We cannot give up!"

The fight had left Hillmaken. He only shook his head.

Eelion roared at him. "No! *You* cannot surrender to these weak creatures."

Hillmaken did not respond but instead collapsed fully onto the beach. He had lost a tremendous amount of blood. Aridin stepped toward the broken lizard and looked down at him with sympathy.

"Tend to him, because he is still our brother. He was not always this way."

Spiders scurried across the beach and assembled around Hillmaken. In a frenzy, they spun fast webs around his wounded tail and leg to stop the bleeding.

Eelion could not accept and believe the king's compassion. "How can you help him now, Aridin? Help the one who sought to overthrow you? The one who ordered your son to be taken? The one who ordered me to take your wing?"

Honu stepped took a step toward him. "The Venom corrupted him, as it corrupted you, Eelion."

"No, the Venom made us strong and powerful!"

"The four of us were there that day the stone fell from the sky, Eelion," Aridin reminded him. "Your power came with a price. The Venom Stone stole away the good that was in you."

"Even then," Eelion hissed, "you and Honu tried to keep its power from us."

Honu shook his head. "We were trying to protect you and Hillmaken. We were all friends once. Do you not remember?"

"I remember you trying to keep this gift of power away from us."

Aridin added, "A power you still underestimate and cannot control."

Eelion was about to reply but stopped when he noticed something slowly moving across the water. Dozens of large floating masses had drifted out from the canyon and were bobbing across the lake. They were giant blobs of the Venom flyers that had drowned in the webby traps—yet another sign of their defeat.

"See? That power did not save your flyers," Honu pointed out.

Eelion hissed as he sidled backward away from the shore and deeper into the lake water.

Honu continued to walk toward him. "It's over, Eelion."

"It's *not* over!" Eelion hissed and then darted out of the water and shot across the beach back into the conversion pool.

The entirety of the beach watched in awe as the four-eyed viper stretched his head up over the Venom Stone, unhinged his jaw, and swallowed it whole. As the stone made its way down his throat, his body convulsed, and two more spider eyes popped out on top of the first.

"Stop! It will kill you, Eelion," Hillmaken pled.

"I am strong, Hillmaken—clearly much stronger than *you* ever were. I will rebuild our armies. Venom will rise again, and we *will* rule the desert."

Eelion did not wait for a reply but sprang back out of the pool and darted back across beach, diving into the lake. He raced across the water, holding his head above the surface, leering back at the Elders. Aridin looked skyward and bellowed out orders to his flyers. Hundreds of falcons, hawks, and owls responded in kind with an affirmative call, then peeled out of the swarm and chased after Eelion as he made his escape. Aridin wanted him captured alive, as there had been enough death this day. The pack of birds converged on Eelion just as he plunged underwater, narrowly avoiding the team of talons trying to snatch him. The birds pulled up and cried out the report of Eelion's disappearance. Other birds joined in the search for him as they circled above the lake.

Aridin stepped into the cool shallows of the lake. "He is gone."

"For now," Honu replied.

Thirty-Nine

The sun had now climbed fully out over the horizon. The distant clouds reflected its warmth in delicate shades of pink and blue. Birds and bugs chirped and buzzed together in a united and joyous song. Aridin summoned them with a long, powerful screech, and the swirling array descended down toward the beach. When the entirety of the swarm had landed, insects and feathered flyers sat, squatted, and squeezed into any open space on and around the Gathering Beach. Insects completely covered the fallen Balancing Stone, and their wings glinted and glittered with pops of sunlight. Branches of ocotillos, mesquites, and ironwoods bowed as birds of all shapes and sizes perched across them.

Olivia circled down with the swarm and landed on the beach in front of Nick and Cade. Her brief happiness disappeared when she realized Sam had not yet made it back.

"Where is Sam?"

Cade looked down and, with pain in his heart, said, "He was taken away from us by some bird—a Venom bird."

"No, Cade. He's alive, and he saved me."

"Wait. What?" Cade asked.

"Yes, he rescued me!"

In unison, Nick's and Cade's ears tuned to a noise coming from the canyon.

"Do you hear that?" Nick asked.

"Another swarm?" Cade responded.

Olivia also looked up, and fear struck her. "A swarm? Oh no. Sam!"

Olivia took flight, and Nick and Cade sprinted through the crowded beach toward the buzzing noise. They cut around the corner of the canyon but stopped in their tracks when they saw a small swarm circling over the river.

"More?" Cade questioned.

Nick pointed. "Look in the water, just below them."

"A reed!" Cade exclaimed.

"Sam!" they yelled in unison.

Aridin heard their cries and let out two rolling screeches. With a buzz and a blur, all of the insects lifted off the Balancing Stone and flew into the canyon. They quickly engulfed the last of Hillmaken's swarm and then flew away into the desert to dispose of them.

Olivia circled over the water as Nick and Cade sprinted upstream along the shoreline. They slowed to a walk and watched as the reed continued to drift in the current of the river. With a splash, Sam exploded out of the water, gasping for air. He frantically looked around, making sure no more Venom flyers were circling over him. He spun in the water, trying to get his bearings. His heart jumped as he heard his name and saw his brothers running toward him.

"Nick! Cade!" he exclaimed.

Sam was smiling from ear to ear as he paddled himself to shore. He'd thought he would never see his brothers again. He gained his footing just as Olivia landed in the shallow water, a split second before Nick and Cade arrived. She threw her wings around Sam's neck.

"You're OK!" She beamed.

"You're OK, too!" He squeezed her back.

Nick and Cade joined their embrace on the riverbank.

"What happened, Sam?" Cade asked.

Olivia answered for Sam. "He rescued me. He is my hero."

"No, you are *my* hero, Olivia. You flew straight into that swarm."

"You're both heroes," Nick added with a smile.

Together, the four of them walked back to the Gathering Beach.

Fourty

A hush fell over all those gathered on the beach, while all eyes were focused on Aridin as he spoke.

"Followers of the light, together with the Old Poem guiding us, we have defeated this threat! We will again have peace in the Desert Realm."

The beach came alive in jubilation. The sound was beautiful to Aridin, who continued, "The Old Poem led us to these brave young heroes, who saved us from the rule of Venom."

All those on the Gathering Beach turned to face Nick, Cade, Sam, and Olivia as they stepped back onto the sand. The Elders welcomed them with loud choruses of celebratory elation. The quartet approached the king and then stopped in front of him and bowed.

"Rise, young ones. We all should be honoring to you."

Honu stood next to Aridin and smiled as he addressed them. "*The three* of the Old Poem, your parents would be so proud of you."

"Like you, they too were heroes in this fight," Aridin added.

The brothers said nothing but only exchanged puzzled glances with one another before turning back to Aridin.

"Yes, your parents sacrificed everything to protect you and fight for peace in our desert—a peace you secured here today."

Cade asked what his brothers were thinking. "What *really* happened to them?"

"That is a long story for another time," Honu replied.

A low, dying voice arose from the crowded beach. "Yes, they were brave, very brave. Like you."

It was Hillmaken, who was recovering in the shadow of the giant stone. His web bandages had stopped the blood loss, but he was still very weak and close to dying. He struggled but managed to claw himself out of the thick, soft sand and back onto his feet. Animals parted a path for him as he slowly made his way toward the Elders.

"You *all* are heroes. You *all* are brave. You defeated an enemy that outnumbered and was more powerful than you. Truly, *now* I see that the Old Poem favors those who follow the light."

Aridin looked down at the once-mighty lizard. "It is not too late to follow the light, Hillmaken."

"How? I have done so much evil."

"Light will always overtake the darkness of evil."

"Look what I did. I sent horrible creatures to attack you in your home. I sent them to steal your child."

"My wife and child are safe now."

"Look what I did to you, Aridin. Your wing—I stole the sky away from you."

"The Venom Stone corrupted you, Hillmaken. Those days can be behind us. I hold no anger toward you."

Hillmaken began to sway as if he was going to collapse, but he steadied himself and continued, "Your compassion has defeated the Venom in me, Aridin."

Aridin clicked out orders. "Tend to him. Take him to the Slot. Its walls will heal him."

"Not yet, my king," Hillmaken pleaded.

Aridin clicked again, halting the two columns of spiders that were to transport Hillmaken.

"Danix!" Hillmaken called, swaying again.

"Yes, Master."

"Come to me. I am giving them the stone."

"Master? Are you sure?"

"To me, Danix."

"Is this about your dream, Master?"

Hillmaken ignored his scorpion's query. "To me, Danix. The Red Stone."

Danix asked no more questions and scurried through the multitude to his leader's side.

"After the first chapter of this war, during the time of my banishment, I searched endlessly for the Venom Stone. I knew Aridin and Honu would hide it well. I went westward in my search, tearing apart the earth as I roamed. Eventually, I reached the ocean. I scoured the coasts for many years, always digging deep and climbing high as I sought the Venom Stone. One morning, I had tasted enough of the wretched salt air and made the decision to take my search away from the shores. I thought perhaps you had decided to hide it in the cold, in the tree-filled Forest Realms of the north.

"I pulled up one last mound of sand, and as I sifted through the wet earth, I felt something. It was a stone; like the Venom Stone, it held power. It was red and was neither a gem nor a rock, but somehow it was like both, and it seemed alive. It tricked my mind into thinking I had found the Venom Stone, and I quickly made plans for my immediate and triumphant return to the Desert Realm."

Hillmaken nodded at Danix, and his loyal scorpion began to tremble as his legs danced and spiked the ground in a blur of panicked movement. He lurched and then stopped, his tail fell flat, and his legs curled up under him. He sat still for several seconds. Then there was a quiet pop, and one of the wide-plated scales in the middle of his back lifted open like a trapdoor. Inside was a hollowed-out compartment that held a jagged red stone.

"Tell him of the dream, Master."

Hillmaken reached into Danix's back and pulled out the Red Stone. He turned and held it out for the group's inspection as he continued.

"Yes, the dream. That night, I burrowed deep in the earth to rest. I believe I finally stopped digging somewhere under the ocean. I fell into a deep slumber as I clutched this new stone. Lucid visions came to me, but somehow they were like dreams within dreams. I saw visions of the Venom Stone as it fell to earth again, when the Old Poem spoke to me."

Hillmaken closed his eyes as he recalled the words that danced in his head that night:

"An unearthed stone, asleep by the ocean,
joined with the two, sets curing in motion.
Balance and Pathway dance with the Red
as life is brought back to what was once dead.
The earth will weave healing of flesh and of bone;
the triad carves life out of sand, mud, and stone."

Honu understood its meaning and spoke with excitement. "Cade, take out the Pathway Stone. Nick, pick up the Balancing Stone. We need it."

Sam sprinted ahead of Nick toward the Balancing Stone. He leaped up and grabbed Zona's shell, which still hung off the tapered end of the giant rock. The shell had snapped shut by the time he landed on the beach with it in his arms. He walked it over to Honu, stooped down, and laid it at his feet.

"Thank you, Sam."

Those gathered watched in silence, disbelief, and awe as Nick approached the Balancing Stone, stood on his tiptoes, and reached for it. A thunderous crack tore through the air when Nick's paws made contact with the boulder. Cold air kicked up from the ground and swirled furiously around the Gathering Beach. The Balancing Stone lifted off the beach, and in a flash, the massive boulder shrank back to the small triangular stone Nick had kept tucked away in his pack. The

Balancing Stone had left a deep and gruesome scar on the beach. Gnarled remains of the Venom army lined its dripping walls. The fallen fighters were unrecognizable.

"Sam, take this," Hillmaken said and offered him the Red Stone.

He hesitated and then slowly reached out for it. "Thank you."

"Boys, gather together, and use all three stones as you did the Pathway."

They once again formed into their triangle. The Elders squeezed in tightly around them, trying to get a closer look. Nick held the Balancing Stone out over their triangle. Cade and Sam followed his lead and extended their arms.

In unison, they counted, "One, two, three."

They each dropped their stones and swung their reeds. The sound was immediate; a sharp knocking resounded out across the beach and over the lake. The stones instantly became blurs as they bounced back and forth against the reeds. The trail of the Red Stone looked like a line of fire.

Cade saw something forming and rising from the middle of their triangle and asked, "What is that?"

"It's not a map. Something is *growing* out of the sand," Nick replied.

Honu looked on and repeated the words Hillmaken had heard in his dream: "The triad carves life…"

The wind continued to whip and circle around them as a form began to take shape inside their triangle. It grew by sucking up sand and dirt from the beach. As the swirling air spread and grew stronger, it pushed the closest of the Elders away from the hares' triangle. Amid the shooting stones and swinging reeds, the sand rolled and swelled like water from a spring, as if it were alive. The form continued to take shape and was beginning to rise up out of the beach.

Honu encouraged them. "Keep going, boys."

They continued to shoot the stones back and forth a dizzying speed. However, their collective focus was squarely on what was forming up out of the rolling sand.

Cade recognized it. "It's a wing!"

Aridin stepped closer to the boys, and the wing of sand rose from the beach and began to float toward him.

"That is enough, boys."

At Honu's command, they stopped their reeds and snatched the stones out of the air, each catching the stone he had originally started with.

The wing was the same size and shape as Aridin's left wing. However, instead of bone, flesh, and feathers, it was made of moving, living earth. The sunlight glittered across the wing as if were water.

The swirling gale carried the wing over to Aridin, and then even harsher winds started up around the beach. In a blur, a tall sand eddy emerged and circled over them, and then it opened up like a bloom, collapsing and engulfing Aridin. For several long seconds, a microstorm spun around him. His silhouette could barely be seen inside the stormy funnel. Then, like the snap of a branch, the wind disappeared, and the sand dropped back down on the beach, revealing the king.

He stood tall and proud, his golden-brown feathers shining like metal in the sun. The wing Eelion and his henchmen had stolen had been restored. He was whole again.

Aridin stepped out over the rise of sand and walked toward Hillmaken. "Thank you, my friend."

"Please do not thank me, Aridin. I have brought so much pain and death to the desert."

"You have begun your walk back to the light. You shared something you did not have to. You have given me back the gift of flight. I will again feel air under my wings; I will again soar over the beautiful desert. I am forever grateful."

For the first time in hundreds of years, Hillmaken felt the power of love, and tears filled his eyes. He said nothing more.

A sharp screech rose from the southern stretch of the beach. Those gathered looked up to see the queen flying toward them, and she was carrying something.

"Aridin, it is time," Honu whispered to his friend.

Sparra carefully held the Oonakestree between her talons as she zoomed toward them. She opened her wings, halting her descent just inches above the ground. She gently placed the egg on the mound of sand where the king's new wing had just materialized.

"Your wing," she declared and then stepped away from the egg and nuzzled up against Aridin. A peaceful look fell over their faces as they looked down at their soon-to-be-born son.

The egg moved, and there was a soft cracking of the shell. Aridin and Sparra drew closer together, their hearts overflowing with happiness. There was another crack. This time, a small yellow beak appeared out of the opening. Tiny flakes of shell popped off as the prince tried to chip open his exit. After several more pokes, the beak stopped.

"Aridin," Sparra whispered to her husband, "should we help?"

"Let him be. He can do it."

Sparra looked up for a bit more reassurance from her husband. "Aridin?"

He looked into her eyes, but before he could reply, there was another crack. They watched as their son broke free from his shell and tumbled out onto the sand. He rolled to a stop near their feet and looked up at them. He wobbled up to standing, almost falling over as he tried to shake the sand out of his soft white down. He steadied himself and stepped into the loving wings of his parents. He had the beak and brow of his mother and the same golden eyes of his father.

"He's beautiful!" Sparra beamed.

"He is, Sparra. He looks just like you," Aridin replied with joy and pride.

Honu extended his long neck up and declared, "The prince of the Desert Realm!"

Howls, chirps, and songs erupted across the beach.

Honu turned to Nick, Cade, Sam, and Olivia. "Your bravery saved the prince and secured the balance of the desert."

"What about Eelion?" Sam asked. "Did he drown?"

Honu looked out across the water and answered, "No, likely not. With that stone in his belly, he could spend hours underwater if he wanted. I suspect he went down to search the depths of the Great Lake. There are believed to be several waterways that lead to other realms. He could be anywhere."

"He swallowed the Venom Stone. That should kill him, right?" Cade added.

"The Venom Stone will not kill him. It needs Eelion now. It knows he is its last chance to take over the desert."

"It *knows?*"

"Yes, the Venom Stone is more than just a rock." Honu paused for a moment. "We should have known when we found it."

"That is enough talk of that for today, my friend," Aridin interjected.

"You are correct, my king. Let us celebrate the birth of your son! What is the name of the new prince?"

"It is Aeto-Koa. It is an ancient word from the Western Island Realm that means 'brave eagle.'"

"It is a fitting name. He will be brave like his father," Sparra added, while keeping her eyes on their son.

"Yes, he will. He has already survived so much," Honu affirmed.

Many of the winged animals took their celebratory songs to flight as the festivity erupted on the beach. The sky was alive with birds, bugs, and bats that danced through the air.

Aridin turned to face the four young heroes. "I am your king, but the Old Poem spoke of you. I am here to serve *you*. The entire Desert Realm owes you much. You saved our prince. You saved *our* son. Look up. You have returned the birds to the skies. You saved us from the dark rule of Venom."

The foursome stood quietly in front of Aridin and could only smile. The kindness and humility of his words were overwhelming. Sam whispered something into Nick's ear, who quickly nodded. He then passed the message along to Cade, who bent down and shared it with Olivia. Then, in unison, the four of them bowed to the royal family.

Before any more words could be spoken, Prince Aeto-Koa stepped away from his parents' protection and walked through the thick sand toward Nick, Cade, and Sam. He looked up at them and let out three high chirps. Then he opened his wings and bowed.

"He knows you rescued him," Sparra said, smiling.

Nick looked at the queen. "We had to save him."

"You *chose* to save him," Honu replied.

"The Old Poem spoke of what was possible. Your actions made those words alive and real," Aridin added.

The young prince looked up at Olivia, squawked again, and then scuttled back over to the embrace of his parents.

Aridin exchanged a knowing glance with Honu and then addressed the four of them. "The Desert Realm may call on you again, young ones."

"Be ready," Honu added.

They would be, indeed.

Made in the USA
Columbia, SC
29 September 2018